PENGUIN TWENTIETH-CENTURY CLASSICS

LOVE AMONG THE HAYSTACKS
AND OTHER STORIES

David Herbert Lawrence was born at Eastwood, Nottingham-shire, in 1885, fourth of the five children of a miner and his middle-class wife. He attended Nottingham High School and Nottingham University College. His first novel, *The White Peacock*, was published in 1911, just a few weeks after the death of his mother to whom he had been abnormally close. At this time he finally ended his relationship with Jessie Chambers (the Miriam of *Sons and Lovers*) and became engaged to Louie Burrows. His career as a schoolteacher was ended in 1911 by the illness which was ultimately diagnosed as tuberculosis.

In 1912 Lawrence eloped to Germany with Frieda Weekley, the German wife of his former modern languages tutor. They were married on their return to England in 1914. Lawrence was now living, precariously, by his writing. His greatest novels, *The Rainbow* and *Women in Love*, were completed in 1915 and 1916. The former was suppressed, and he could not find a publisher for the latter.

After the war Lawrence began his 'savage pilgrimage' in search of a more fulfilling mode of life than industrial Western civiliza-tion could offer. This took him to Sicily, Ceylon, Australia and, finally, New Mexico. The Lawrences returned to Europe in 1925. Lawrence's last novel, *Lady Chatterley's Lover*, was banned in 1928, and his paintings confiscated in 1929. He died in Vence in 1930 at the age of forty-four.

Lawrence spent most of his short life living. Nevertheless he produced an amazing quantity of work – novels, stories, poems, plays, essays, travel books, translations, and letters ... After his death Frieda wrote: 'What he had seen and felt and known he gave in his writing to his fellow men, the splendour of living, the hope of more and more life ... a heroic and immeasurable gift.'

D. H. LAWRENCE

Love Among the Haystacks
AND OTHER STORIES

PENGUIN BOOKS

PENGUIN BOOKS

Published by the Penguin Group
Penguin Books Ltd, 27 Wrights Lane, London W8 5TZ, England
Penguin Books USA Inc., 375 Hudson Street, New York, New York 10014, USA
Penguin Books Australia Ltd, Ringwood, Victoria, Australia
Penguin Books Canada Ltd, 10 Alcorn Avenue, Toronto, Ontario, Canada M4V 3B2
Penguin Books (NZ) Ltd, 182–190 Wairau Road, Auckland 10, New Zealand

Penguin Books Ltd, Registered Offices: Harmondsworth, Middlesex, England

'Love Among the Haystacks' was first published in 1930,
'The Lovely Lady' in 1933, 'Rawdon's Roof' in 1928,
'The Rocking-Horse Winner' in *The Ghost Book*, edited by Cynthia Asquith, in 1926,
'The Man Who Loved Islands' in America (in the collection *The Woman Who Rode Away*)
in 1929, and 'The Man Who Died' (originally 'The Escaped Cock') in 1929

First published in Penguin Books 1960
23 25 27 29 30 28 26 24 22

Also available in Canada in a Viking/Compass edition together with
The Ladybird, The Fox and *The Captain's Doll*

Printed in England by Clays Ltd, St Ives plc
Set in Monotype Garamond

CONTENTS

Love Among the Haystacks

I

THE two large fields lay on a hillside facing south. Being newly cleared of hay, they were golden green, and they shone almost blindingly in the sunlight. Across the hill, half-way up, ran a high hedge, that flung its black shadow finely across the molten glow of the sward. The stack was being built just above the hedge. It was of great size, massive, but so silvery and delicately bright in tone that it seemed not to have weight. It rose dishevelled and radiant among the steady, golden-green glare of the field. A little farther back was another, finished stack.

The empty wagon was just passing through the gap in the hedge. From the far-off corner of the bottom field, where the sward was still striped grey with winrows, the loaded wagon launched forward to climb the hill to the stack. The white dots of the hay-makers showed distinctly among the hay.

The two brothers were having a moment's rest, waiting for the load to come up. They stood wiping their brows with their arms, sighing from the heat and the labour of placing the last load. The stack they rode was high, lifting them up above the hedge-tops, and very broad, a great slightly-hollowed vessel into which the sunlight poured, in which the hot, sweet scent of hay was suffocating. Small and inefficacious the brothers looked, half-submerged in the loose, great trough, lifted high up as if on an altar reared to the sun.

Maurice, the younger brother, was a handsome young fellow of twenty-one, careless and debonair, and full of vigour. His grey eyes, as he taunted his brother, were bright and baffled with a strong emotion. His swarthy face had the same peculiar smile, expectant and glad and nervous, of a young man roused for the first time in passion.

'Tha sees,' he said, as he leaned on the pommel of his fork, 'tha thowt as tha'd done me one, didna ter?' He smiled as he spoke, then fell again into his pleasant torment of musing.

'I thought nowt – tha knows so much,' retorted Geoffrey, with the touch of a sneer. His brother had the better of him. Geoffrey was a very heavy, hulking fellow, a year older than Maurice. His blue eyes were unsteady, they glanced away quickly; his mouth was morbidly sensitive. One felt him wince away, through the whole of his great body. His inflamed self-consciousness was a disease in him.

'Ah, but though, I know tha did,' mocked Maurice. 'Tha went slinkin' off' – Geoffrey winced convulsively – 'thinking as that wor the last night as any of us'ud ha'e ter stop here, an' so tha'd leave me to sleep out, though it wor thy turn –'

He smiled to himself, thinking of the result of Geoffrey's ruse.

'I didna go slinkin' off neither,' retorted Geoffrey, in his heavy, clumsy manner, wincing at the phrase. 'Didna my feyther send me to fetch some coal –'

'Oh yes, oh yes – we know all about it. But tha sees what tha missed, my lad.'

Maurice, chuckling, threw himself on his back in the bed of hay. There was absolutely nothing in his world, then, except the shallow ramparts of the stack, and the blazing sky. He clenched his fists tight, threw his arms across his face, and braced his muscles again. He was evidently very much moved, so acutely that it was hardly pleasant, though he still smiled. Geoffrey, standing behind him, could just see his red mouth, with the young moustache like black fur, curling back and showing the teeth in a smile. The elder brother leaned his chin on the pommel of his fork, looking out across the country.

Far away was the faint blue heap of Nottingham. Between, the country lay under a haze of heat, with here and there a flag of colliery smoke waving. But near at hand, at the foot of the hill, across the deep-hedged high road, was only the silence of the old church and the castle farm, among their trees. The large view only made Geoffrey more sick. He looked away, to the wagons crossing the field below him, the empty cart like a big insect moving down-hill, the load coming up, rocking like a ship, the brown head of the horse ducking, the brown knees lifted and planted strenuously. Geoffrey wished it would be quick.

'Tha didna think –'

Geoffrey started, coiled within himself, and looked down at the handsome lips moving in speech below the brown arms of his brother.

'Tha didna think 'er'd be thur wi' me – or tha wouldna ha' left me to it,' Maurice said, ending with a little laugh of excited memory. Geoffrey flushed with hate, and had an impulse to set his foot on that moving, taunting mouth, which was there below him. There was silence for a time, then, in a peculiar tone of delight, Maurice's voice came again, spelling out the words, as it were:

> '*Ich bin klein, mein Herz ist rein,*
> *Ist niemand d'rin als Christ allein.*'

Maurice chuckled, then, convulsed at a twinge of recollection, keen as pain, he twisted over, pressed himself into the hay.

'Can thee say thy prayers in German?' came his muffled voice.

'I non want,' growled Geoffrey.

Maurice chuckled. His face was quite hidden, and in the dark he was going over again his last night's experiences.

'What about kissing 'er under th' ear, Sonny,' he said, in a curious, uneasy tone. He writhed, still startled and inflamed by his first contact with love.

Geoffrey's heart swelled within him, and things went dark. He could not see the landscape.

'An' there's just a nice two-handful of her bosom,' came the low, provocative tones of Maurice, who seemed to be talking to himself.

The two brothers were both fiercely shy of women, and until this hay harvest, the whole feminine sex had been represented by their mother and in presence of any other women they were dumb louts. Moreover, brought up by a proud mother, a stranger in the country, they held the common girls as beneath them, because beneath their mother, who spoke pure English, and was very quiet. Loud-mouthed and broad-tongued the common girls were. So these two young men had grown up virgin but tormented.

Now again Maurice had the start of Geoffrey, and the elder brother was deeply mortified. There was a danger of his sinking into a morbid state, from sheer lack of living, lack of interest. The foreign governess at the Vicarage, whose garden lay beside the top field, had talked to the lads through the hedge, and had fascinated them. There was a great elder bush, with its broad creamy flowers crumbling on to the garden path, and into the field. Geoffrey never smelled elder-flower without starting and wincing, thinking of the strange foreign voice that had so startled him as he mowed out with the scythe in the hedge bottom. A baby had run through the gap, and the Fräulein, calling in German, had come brushing down the flowers in pursuit. She had started so on seeing a man standing there in the shade, that for a moment she could not move: and then she had blundered into the rake which was lying by his side. Geoffrey, forgetting she was a woman when he saw her pitch forward, had picked her up carefully, asking: 'Have you hurt you?'

Then she had broken into a laugh, and answered in German, showing him her arms, and knitting her brows. She was nettled rather badly.

'You want a dock leaf,' he said. She frowned in a puzzled fashion.

'A dock leaf?' she repeated. He had rubbed her arms with the green leaf.

And now, she had taken to Maurice. She had seemed to prefer himself at first. Now she had sat with Maurice in the moonlight, and had let him kiss her. Geoffrey sullenly suffered, making no fight.

Unconsciously, he was looking at the Vicarage garden. There she was, in a golden-brown dress. He took off his hat, and held up his right hand in greeting to her. She, a small, golden figure, waved her hand negligently from among the potato rows. He remained, arrested, in the same posture, his hat in his left hand, his right arm upraised, thinking. He could tell by the negligence of her greeting that she was waiting for Maurice. What did she think of himself? Why wouldn't she have him?

Hearing the voice of the wagoner leading the load, Maurice rose. Geoffrey still stood in the same way, but his face was sullen, and his upraised hand was slack with brooding. Maurice faced up-hill. His eyes lit up and he laughed. Geoffrey dropped his own arm, watching.

'Lad!' chuckled Maurice. 'I non knowed 'er wor there.' He waved his hand clumsily. In these matters Geoffrey did better. The elder brother watched the girl. She ran to the end of the path, behind the bushes, so that she was screened from the house. Then she waved her handkerchief wildly. Maurice did not notice the manoeuvre. There was the cry of a child. The girl's figure vanished, reappeared holding up a white childish bundle, and came down the path. There she put down her charge, sped up-hill to a great ash tree, climbed quickly to a large horizontal bar that formed the fence there, and, standing poised, blew kisses with both her hands, in a foreign fashion that excited the brothers. Maurice laughed aloud, as he waved his red handkerchief.

'Well, what's the danger?' shouted a mocking voice from below. Maurice collapsed, blushing furiously.

'Nowt!' he called.

There was a hearty laugh from below.

The load rode up, sheered with a hiss against the stack, then sank back again upon the scotches. The brothers ploughed across the mass of hay, taking the forks. Presently a big burly man, red and glistening, climbed to the top of the load. Then he turned round, scrutinized the hillside from under his shaggy brows. He caught sight of the girl under the ash tree.

'Oh, that's who it is,' he laughed. 'I thought it was some such bird, but I couldn't see her.'

The father laughed in a hearty, chaffing way, then began to teem the load. Geoffrey, on the stack above, received his great forkfuls, and swung them over to Maurice, who took them, placed them, building the stack. In the intense sunlight, the three worked in silence, knit together in a brief passion of work. The father stirred slowly for a moment, getting the hay from under his feet. Geoffrey waited, the blue tines of his fork glittering in expectation: the mass rose, his fork swung beneath it, there was a light clash of blades, then the hay was swept on to the stack, caught by Maurice, who placed it judiciously. One after another, the shoulders of the three men bowed and braced themselves. All wore light blue, bleached shirts, that stuck close to their backs. The father moved mechanically, his thick, rounded shoulders bending and lifting dully: he worked monotonously. Geoffrey flung away his strength. His massive shoulders swept and flung the hay extravagantly.

'Dost want to knock me ower?' asked Maurice angrily. He had to brace himself against the impact. The three men worked intensely, as if some will urged them. Maurice was light and swift at the work, but he had to use his judgement. Also, when he has to place the hay along the far ends, he had some distance to carry it. So he was too slow for Geoffrey. Ordinarily, the elder would have placed the hay as far as possible where his brother wanted it. Now, however, he pitched his forkfuls into the middle of the stack. Maurice strode swiftly and handsomely across the bed, but the work was too much for him. The other two men, clenched in their receive and deliver, kept up a high pitch of labour. Geoffrey still flung the hay at random. Maurice was perspiring heavily with heat and exertion, and was getting worried. Now and again, Geoffrey wiped his arm across his brow, mechanically, like a animal. Then he glanced with satisfaction at Maurice's moiled condition, and caught the next forkful.

'Wheer dost think thou'rt hollin' it, fool!' panted Maurice, as his brother flung a forkful out of reach.

'Wheer I've a mind,' answered Geoffrey.

Maurice toiled on, now very angry. He felt the sweat trickling down his body: drops fell into his long black lashes, blinding him, so that he had to stop and angrily dash his eyes clear. The veins stood out in his swarthy neck. He felt he would burst, or drop, if the work did not soon slacken off. He heard his father's fork dully scrape the cart bottom.

'There, the last,' the father panted. Geoffrey tossed the last light lot at random, took off his hat, and, steaming in the sunshine as he wiped himself, stood complacently watching Maurice struggle with clearing the bed.

'Don't you think you've got your bottom corner a bit far out?' came the father's voice from below. 'You'd better be drawing in now, hadn't you?'

'I thought you said next load,' Maurice called sulkily.

'Aye! All right. But isn't this bottom corner – ?'

Maurice, impatient, took no notice.

Geoffrey strode over the stack, and stuck his fork in the offending corner. 'What – here?' he bawled in his great voice.

'Aye – isn't it a bit loose?' came the irritating voice.

Geoffrey pushed his fork in the jutting corner, and, leaning his weight on the handle, shoved. He thought it shook. He thrust again with all his power. The mass swayed.

'What art up to, tha fool!' cried Maurice, in a high voice.

'Mind who tha'rt callin' a fool,' said Geoffrey, and he prepared to push again. Maurice sprang across, and elbowed his brother aside. On the yielding, swaying bed of hay, Geoffrey lost his foothold and fell grovelling. Maurice tried the corner.

'It's solid enough,' he shouted angrily.

'Aye – all right,' came the conciliatory voice of the father; 'you do get a bit of rest now there's such a long way to cart it,' he added reflectively.

Geoffrey had got to his feet.

'Tha'll mind who tha'rt nudging, I can tell thee,' he threatened heavily; adding, as Maurice continued to work, 'an' tha non ca's him a fool again, dost hear?'

'Not till next time,' sneered Maurice.

As he worked silently round the stack, he neared where his brother stood like a sullen statue, leaning on his fork-handle, looking out over the countryside. Maurice's heart quickened in its beat. He worked forward, until a point of his fork

caught in the leather of Geoffrey's boot, and the metal rang
sharply.

'Are ter going ta shift thysen?' asked Maurice threaten-
ingly. There was no reply from the great block. Maurice
lifted his upper lip like a dog. Then he put out his elbow
and tried to push his brother into the stack, clear of his way.

'Who are ter shovin'?' came the deep, dangerous voice.

'Thaïgh,' replied Maurice, with a sneer, and straightway
the two brothers set themselves against each other, like
opposing bulls, Maurice trying his hardest to shift Geoffrey
from his footing, Geoffrey leaning all his weight in resistance.
Maurice, insecure in his footing, staggered a little, and
Geoffrey's weight followed him. He went slithering over the
edge of the stack.

Geoffrey turned white to the lips, and remained standing,
listening. He heard the fall. Then a flush of darkness came
over him, and he remained standing only because he was
planted. He had not strength to move. He could hear no
sound from below, was only faintly aware of a sharp shriek
from a long way off. He listened again. Then he filled with
sudden panic.

'Feyther!' he roared, in his tremendous voice: 'Feyther!
Feyther!'

The valley re-echoed with the sound. Small cattle on the
hillside looked up. Men's figures came running from the
bottom field, and much nearer a woman's figure was racing
across the upper field. Geoffrey waited in terrible suspense.

'Ah-h!' he heard the strange, wild voice of the girl cry
out. 'Ah-h!' – and then some foreign wailing speech. Then:
'Ah-h! Are you dea-ed!'

He stood sullenly erect on the stack, not daring to go down,
longing to hide in the hay, but too sullen to stoop out of
sight. He heard his eldest brother come up, panting:

'Whatever's amiss!' and then the labourer, and then his
father.

'Whatever have you been doing?' he heard his father ask,
while yet he had not come round the corner of the stack.
And then, in a low, bitter tone:

'Eh, he's done for! I'd no business to ha' put it all on that stack.'

There was a moment or two of silence, then the voice of Henry, the eldest brother, said crisply:

'He's not dead – he's coming round.'

Geoffrey heard, but was not glad. He had as lief Maurice were dead. At least that would be final: better than meeting his brother's charges, and of seeing his mother pass to the sick-room. If Maurice was killed, he himself would not explain, no, not a word, and they could hang him if they liked. If Maurice were only hurt, then everybody would know, and Geoffrey could never lift his face again. What added torture, to pass along, everybody knowing. He wanted something that he could stand back to, something definite, if it were only the knowledge that he had killed his brother. He *must* have something firm to back up to, or he would go mad. He was so lonely, he who above all needed the support of sympathy.

'No, he's commin' to; I tell you he is,' said the labourer.

'He's not dea-ed, he's not dea-ed,' came the passionate, strange sing-song of the foreign girl. 'He's not dead – no-o.'

'He wants some brandy – look at the colour of his lips,' said the crisp, cold voice of Henry. 'Can you fetch some?'

'Wha-at? Fetch?' Fräulein did not understand.

'Brandy,' said Henry, very distinct.

'Brrandy!' she re-echoed.

'You go, Bill,' groaned the father.

'Aye, I'll go,' replied Bill, and he ran across the field.

Maurice was not dead, nor going to die. This Geoffrey now realized. He was glad after all that the extreme penalty was revoked. But he hated to think of himself going on. He would always shrink now. He had hoped and hoped for the time when he would be careless, bold as Maurice, when he would not wince and shrink. Now he would always be the same, coiling up in himself like a tortoise with no shell.

'Ah-h! He's getting better!' came the wild voice of the Fräulein, and she began to cry, a strange sound, that startled the men, made the animal bristle within them. Geoffrey shuddered as he heard, between her sobbing, the impatient moaning of his brother as the breath came back.

The labourer returned at a run, followed by the Vicar. After the brandy, Maurice made more moaning, hiccuping noise. Geoffrey listened in torture. He heard the Vicar asking for explanations. All the united, anxious voices replied in brief phrases.

'It was that other,' cried the Fräulein. 'He knocked him over – Ha!'

She was shrill and vindictive.

'I don't think so,' said the father to the Vicar, in a quite audible but private tone, speaking as if the Fräulein did not understand his English.

The Vicar addressed his children's governess in bad German. She replied in a torrent which he would not confess was too much for him. Maurice was making little moaning, sighing noises.

'Where's your pain, boy, eh?' the father asked pathetically.

'Leave him alone a bit,' came the cool voice of Henry. 'He's winded, if no more.'

'You'd better see that no bones are broken,' said the anxious Vicar.

'It wor a blessing as he should a dropped on that heap of hay just there,' said the labourer. 'If he'd happened to ha' catched hisself on this nog o' wood 'e wouldna ha' stood much chance.'

Geoffrey wondered when he would have courage to venture down. He had wild notions of pitching himself head foremost from the stack: if he could only extinguish himself, he would be safe. Quite frantically, he longed not to be. The idea of going through life thus coiled up within himself in morbid self-consciousness, always lonely, surly, and a misery, was enough to make him cry out. What would they all think when they knew he had knocked Maurice off that high stack?

They were talking to Maurice down below. The lad had recovered in great measure, and was able to answer faintly.

'Whatever was you doin'?' the father asked gently. 'Was

16

you playing about with our Geoffrey? – Aye, and where
is he?'

Geoffrey's heart stood still.

'I dunno,' said Henry, in a curious, ironic tone.

'Go an' have a look,' pleaded the father, infinitely relieved
over one son, anxious now concerning the other. Geoffrey
could not bear that his eldest brother should climb up and
question him in his high-pitched drawl of curiosity. The
culprit doggedly set his feet on the ladder. His nailed boots
slipped a rung.

'Mind yourself,' shouted the over-wrought father.

Geoffrey stood like a criminal at the foot of the ladder,
glancing furtively at the group. Maurice was lying, pale and
slightly convulsed, upon a heap of hay. The Fräulein was
kneeling beside his head. The Vicar had the lad's shirt full
open down the breast, and was feeling for broken ribs. The
father kneeled on the other side, the labourer and Henry
stood aside.

'I can't find anything broken,' said the Vicar, and he
sounded slightly disappointed.

'There's nowt broken to find,' murmured Maurice, smiling.

The father started. 'Eh?' he said. 'Eh?' and he bent over
the invalid.

'I say it's not hurt me,' repeated Maurice.

'What were you doing?' asked the cold, ironic voice of
Henry. Geoffrey turned his head away: he had not yet raised
his face.

'Nowt as I know on,' he muttered in a surly tone.

'Why!' cried Fräulein in a reproachful tone. 'I see him –
knock him over!' She made a fierce gesture with her elbow.
Henry curled his long moustache sardonically.

'Nay lass, niver,' smiled the wan Maurice. 'He was fur
enough away from me when I slipped.'

'Oh, ah!' cried the Fräulein, not understanding.

'Yi,' smiled Maurice indulgently.

'I think you're mistaken,' said the father, rather pat. hetic-
ally, smiling at the girl as if she were 'wanting'.

'Oh no,' she cried. 'I *see* him.'

17

'Nay, lass,' smiled Maurice quietly.

She was a Pole, named Paula Jablonowsky: young, only twenty years old, swift and light as a wild cat, with a strange, wild-cat way of grinning. Her hair was blonde and full of life, all crisped into many tendrils with vitality, shaking round her face. Her fine blue eyes were peculiarly lidded, and she seemed to look piercingly, then languorously, like a wild cat. She had somewhat Slavonic cheek-bones, and was very much freckled. It was evident that the Vicar, a pale, rather cold man, hated her.

Maurice lay pale and smiling in her lap, whilst she cleaved to him like a mate. One felt instinctively that they were mated. She was ready at any minute to fight with ferocity in his defence, now he was hurt. Her looks at Geoffrey were full of fierceness. She bowed over Maurice and caressed him with her foreign-sounding English.

'You say what you lai-ike,' she laughed, giving him lordship over her.

'Hadn't you better be going and looking what has become of Margery?' asked the Vicar in tones of reprimand.

'She is with her mother – I heared her. I will go in a whai-ile,' smiled the girl coolly.

'Do you feel as if you could stand?' asked the father, still anxiously.

'Aye, in a bit,' smiled Maurice.

'You want to get up?' caressed the girl, bowing over him, till her face was not far from his.

'I'm in no hurry,' he replied, smiling brilliantly.

This accident had given him quite a strange new ease, an authority. He felt extraordinarily glad. New power had come to him all at once.

'You in no hurry,' she repeated, gathering his meaning. She smiled tenderly: she was in his service.

'She leaves us in another month – Mrs Inwood could stand no more of her,' apologized the Vicar quietly to the father.

'Why, is she – '

'Like a wild thing – disobedient and insolent.'

'Ha!'

The father sounded abstract.

'No more foreign governesses for me.'

Maurice stirred, and looked up at the girl.

'You stand up?' she asked brightly. 'You well?'

He laughed again, showing his teeth winsomely. She lifted his head, sprang to her feet, her hands still holding his head, then she took him under the armpits and had him on his feet before anyone could help. He was much taller than she. He grasped her strong shoulders heavily, leaned against her, and, feeling her round, firm breast doubled up against his side, he smiled, catching his breath.

'You see, I'm all right,' he gasped. 'I was only winded.'

'You all raïght?' she cried, in great glee.

'Yes, I am.'

He walked a few steps after a moment.

'There's nowt ails me, father,' he laughed.

'Quite well, you?' she cried in a pleading tone. He laughed outright, looked down at her, touching her cheek with his fingers.

'That's it – if tha likes.'

'If I lai-ike!' she repeated, radiant.

'She's going at the end of three weeks,' said the Vicar consolingly to the farmer.

2

While they were talking, they heard the far-off hooting of a pit.

'There goes th' loose 'a,' said Henry coldly. 'We're *not* going to get that corner up today.'

The father looked round anxiously.

'Now, Maurice, are you sure you're all right?' he asked.

'Yes, I'm all right. Haven't I told you?'

'Then you sit down there, and in a bit you can be getting dinner out. Henry, you go on the stack. Wheer's Jim? Oh, he's minding the hosses. Bill, and you, Geoffrey, you can pick while Jim loads.'

Maurice sat down under the wych elm to recover. The

Fräulein had fled back. He made up his mind to ask her to marry him. He had got fifty pounds of his own, and his mother would help him. For a long time he sat musing, thinking what he would do. Then, from the float he fetched a big basket covered with a cloth, and spread the dinner. There was an immense rabbit-pie, a dish of cold potatoes, much bread, a great piece of cheese, and a solid rice pudding.

These two fields were four miles from the home farm. But they had been in the hands of the Wookeys for several generations, therefore the father kept them on, and everyone looked forward to the hay harvest at Greasley: it was a kind of picnic. They brought dinner and tea in the milk-float, which the father drove over in the morning. The lads and the labourers cycled. Off and on, the harvest lasted a fortnight. As the high road from Alfreton to Nottingham ran at the foot of the fields, someone usually slept in the hay under the shed to guard the tools. The sons took it in turns. They did not care for it much, and were for that reason anxious to finish the harvest on this day. But work went slack and disjointed after Maurice's accident.

When the load was teemed, they gathered round the white cloth, which was spread under a tree between the hedge and the stack, and, sitting on the ground, ate their meal. Mrs Wookey sent always a clean cloth, and knives and forks and plates for everybody. Mr Wookey was always rather proud of this spread: everything was so proper.

'There now,' he said, sitting down jovially. 'Doesn't this look nice now – eh?'

They all sat round the white spread, in the shadow of the tree and the stack, and looked out up the fields as they ate. From their shady coolness, the gold sward seemed liquid, molten with heat. The horse with the empty wagon wandered a few yards, then stood feeding. Everything was still as a trance. Now and again, the horse between the shafts of the load that stood propped beside the stack, jingled his loose bit as he ate. The men ate and drank in silence, the father reading the newspaper, Maurice leaning back on a saddle, Henry reading the *Nation*, the others eating busily.

Presently 'Helloa! 'Er's 'ere again!' exclaimed Bill. All looked up. Paula was coming across the field carrying a plate.

'She's bringing something to tempt your appetite, Maurice,' said the eldest brother ironically. Maurice was midway through a large wedge of rabbit-pie and some cold potatoes.

'Aye, bless me if she's not,' laughed the father. 'Put that away, Maurice, it's a shame to disappoint her.'

Maurice looked round very shamefaced, not knowing what to do with his plate.

'Give it over here,' said Bill. 'I'll polish him off.'

'Bringing something for the invalid?' laughed the father to the Fräulein. 'He's looking up nicely.'

'I bring him some chicken, him!' She nodded her head at Maurice childishly. He flushed and smiled.

'Tha doesna mean ter bust 'im,' said Bill.

Everybody laughed aloud. The girl did not understand, so she laughed also. Maurice ate his portion very sheepishly.

The father pitied his son's shyness.

'Come here and sit by me,' he said. 'Eh, Fräulein! Is that what they call you?'

'I sit by you, father,' she said innocently.

Henry threw his head back and laughed long and noiselessly.

She settled near to the big, handsome man.

'My name,' she said, 'is Paula Jablonowsky.'

'Is what?' said the father, and the other men went into roars of laughter.

'Tell me again,' said the father. 'Your name –'

'Paula.'

'Paula? Oh – well, it's a rum sort of name, eh? His name –' he nodded at his son.

'Maurice – I know.' She pronounced it sweetly, then laughed into the father's eyes. Maurice blushed to the roots of his hair.

They questioned her concerning her history, and made out that she came from Hanover, that her father was a shopkeeper, and that she had run away from home because she did not like her father. She had gone to Paris.

'Oh,' said the father, now dubious. 'And what did you do there?'

'In school – in a young ladies' school.'

'Did you like it?'

'Oh no – no laïfe – no life!'

'What?'

'When we go out – two and two – all together – no more. Ah, no life, no life.'

'Well, that's a winder!' exclaimed the father. 'No life in Paris! And have you found much life in England?'

'No – ah no. I don't like it.' She made a grimace at the Vicarage.

'How long have you been in England?'

'Chreestmas – so.'

'And what will you do?'

'I will go to London, or to Paris. Ah, Paris! – Or get married!' She laughed into the father's eyes.

The father laughed heartily.

'Get married, eh? And who to?'

'I don't know. I am going away.'

'The country's too quiet for you?' asked the father.

'Too quiet – hm!' she nodded in assent.

'You wouldn't care for making butter and cheese?'

'Making butter – hm!' She turned to him with a glad, bright gesture. 'I like it.'

'Oh,' laughed the father. 'You would, would you?'

She nodded vehemently, with glowing eyes.

'She'd like anything in the shape of a change,' said Henry judicially.

'I think she would,' agreed the father. It did not occur to them that she fully understood what they said. She looked at them closely, then thought with bowed head.

'Hullo!' exclaimed Henry, the alert. A tramp was slouching towards them through the gap. He was a very seedy, slinking fellow, with a tang of horsey braggadocio about him. Small, thin, and ferrety, with a week's red beard bristling on his pointed chin, he came slouching forward.

'Have yer got a bit of a job goin'?' he asked.

'A bit of a job,' repeated the father. 'Why, can't you see as we've a'most done?'

'Aye – but I noticed you was a hand short, an' I thowt as 'appen you'd gie me half a day.'

'What, are *you* any good in a hay close?' asked Henry, with a sneer.

The man stood slouching against the haystack. All the others were seated on the floor. He had an advantage.

'I could work aside any on yer,' he bragged.

'Tha looks it,' laughed Bill.

'And what's your regular trade?' asked the father.

'I'm a jockey by rights. But I did a bit o' dirty work for a boss o' mine, an' I was landed. 'E got the benefit, *I* got kicked out. 'E axed me – an' then 'e looked as if 'e'd never seed me.'

'Did he, though!' exclaimed the father sympathetically.

''E did that!' asserted the man.

'But we've got nothing for you,' said Henry coldly.

'What does the boss say?' asked the man, impudent.

'No, we've no work you can do,' said the father. 'You can have a bit o' something to eat, if you like.'

'I should be glad of it,' said the man.

He was given the chunk of rabbit-pie that remained. This he ate greedily. There was something debased, parasitic, about him, which disgusted Henry. The others regarded him as a curiosity.

'That was nice and tasty,' said the tramp, with gusto.

'Do you want a piece of bread 'n' cheese?' asked the father.

'It'll help to fill up,' was the reply.

The man ate this more slowly. The company was embarrassed by his presence, and could not talk. All the men lit their pipes, the meal over.

'So you dunna want any help?' said the tramp at last.

'No – we can manage what bit there is to do.'

'You don't happen to have a fill of bacca to spare, do you?'

The father gave him a good pinch.

'You're all right here,' he said, looking round. They resented this familiarity. However, he filled his clay pipe and smoked with the rest.

As they were sitting silent, another figure came through the gap in the hedge, and noiselessly approached. It was a woman. She was rather small and finely made. Her face was small, very ruddy, and comely, save for the look of bitterness and aloofness that it wore. Her hair was drawn tightly back under a sailor hat. She gave an impression of cleanness, of precision and directness.

'Have you got some work?' she asked of her man. She ignored the rest. He tucked his tail between his legs.

'No, they haven't got no work for me. They've just gave me a draw of bacca.'

He was a mean crawl of a man.

'An' am I goin' to wait for you out there on the lane all day?'

'You needn't if you don't like. You could go on.'

'Well, are you coming?' she asked contemptuously. He rose to his feet in a rickety fashion.

'You needn't be in such a mighty hurry,' he said. 'If you'd wait a bit you might get summat.'

She glanced for the first time over the men. She was quite young, and would have been pretty, were she not so hard and callous-looking.

'Have you had your dinner?' asked the father.

She looked at him with a kind of anger and turned away. Her face was so childish in its contours, contrasting strangely with her expression.

'Are you coming?' she said to the man.

'He's had his tuck-in. Have a bit, if you want it,' coaxed the father.

'What have you had?' she flashed to the man.

'He's had all what was left o' th' rabbit-pie,' said Geoffrey, in an indignant, mocking tone, 'and a great hunk o' bread an' cheese.'

'Well, it was gave me,' said the man.

The young woman looked at Geoffrey, and he at her. There

was a sort of kinship between them. Both were at odds with
the world. Geoffrey smiled satirically. She was too grave,
too deeply incensed even to smile.

'There's a cake here, though – you can have a bit o' that,'
said Maurice blithely.

She eyed him with scorn.

Again she looked at Geoffrey. He seemed to understand
her. She turned, and in silence departed. The man remained
obstinately sucking at his pipe. Everybody looked at him
with hostility.

'We'll be getting to work,' said Henry, rising, pulling off
his coat. Paula got to her feet. She was a little bit confused
by the presence of the tramp.

'I go,' she said, smiling brilliantly. Maurice rose and
followed her sheepishly.

'A good grind, eh?' said the tramp, nodding after the Fräulein. The men only half understood him, but they hated him.

'Hadn't you better be getting off?' said Henry.

The man rose obediently. He was all slouching, parasitic
insolence. Geoffrey loathed him, longed to exterminate him.
He was exactly the worst foe of the hypersensitive: insolence
without sensibility, preying on sensibility.

'Aren't you goin' to give me summat for her? It's nowt
she's had all day, to my knowin'. She'll 'appen eat it if I
take it 'er – though she gets more than I've any knowledge
of' – this with a lewd wink of jealous spite. 'And then tries
to keep a tight hand on me,' he sneered, taking the bread and
cheese, and stuffing it in his pocket.

3

Geoffrey worked sullenly all the afternoon, and Maurice
did the horse-raking. It was exceedingly hot. So the day
wore on, the atmosphere thickened, and the sunlight grew
blurred. Geoffrey was picking with Bill – helping to load the
wagons from the winrows. He was sulky, though extraordinarily relieved: Maurice would not tell. Since the quarrel

neither brother had spoken to the other. But their silence was entirely amicable, almost affectionate. They had both been deeply moved, so much so that their ordinary inter-course was interrupted: but underneath, each felt a strong regard for the other. Maurice was peculiarly happy, his feel-ing of affection swimming over everything. But Geoffrey was still sullenly hostile to the most part of the world. He felt isolated. The free and easy inter-communication between the other workers left him distinctly alone. And he was a man who could not bear to stand alone, he was too much afraid of the vast confusion of life surrounding him, in which he was helpless. Geoffrey mistrusted himself with every-body.

The work went on slowly. It was unbearably hot, and everyone was disheartened.

'We s'll have getting-on-for another day of it,' said the father at tea-time, as they sat under the tree.

'Quite a day,' said Henry.

'Somebody'll have to stop, then,' said Geoffrey. 'It 'ud better be me.'

'Nay, lad, I'll stop,' said Maurice, and he hid his head in confusion.

'Stop again tonight!' exclaimed the father. 'I'd rather you went home.'

'Nay, I'm stoppin',' protested Maurice.

'He wants to do his courting,' Henry enlightened them.

The father thought seriously about it.

'I don't know . . .' he mused, rather perturbed.

But Maurice stayed. Towards eight o'clock, after sun-down, the men mounted their bicycles, the father put the horse in the float, and all departed. Maurice stood in the gap of the hedge and watched them go, the cart rolling and swing-ing down-hill, over the grass stubble, the cyclists dipping swiftly like shadows in front. All passed through the gate, there was a quick clatter of hoofs on the roadway under the lime trees, and they were gone. The young man was very much excited, almost afraid, at finding himself alone.

Darkness was rising from the valley. Already, up the steep

hill the cart-lamps crept indecisively, and the cottage windows were lit. Everything looked strange to Maurice, as if he had not seen it before. Down the hedge a large lime tree teemed with scent that seemed almost like a voice speaking. It startled him. He caught a breath of the over-sweet fragrance, then stood still, listening expectantly.

Up-hill, a horse whinneyed. It was the young mare. The heavy horses went thundering across to the far hedge.

Maurice wondered what to do. He wandered round the deserted stacks restlessly. Heat came in wafts, in thick strands. The evening was a long time cooling. He thought he would g⌐ and wash himself. There was a trough of pure water in the hedge bottom. It was filled by a tiny spring that filtered over the brim of the trough down the lush hedge bottom of the lower field. All round the trough, in the upper field, the land was marshy, and there the meadow-sweet stood like clots of mist, very sickly-smelling in the twilight. The night did not darken, for the moon was in the sky, so that as the tawny colour drew off the heavens they remained pallid with a dimmed moon. The purple bell-flowers in the hedge went black, the ragged robin turned its pink to a faded white, the meadow-sweet gathered light as if it were phosphorescent, and it made the air ache with scent.

Maurice kneeled on the slab of stone bathing his hands and arms, then his face. The water was deliciously cool. He had still an hour before Paula would come: she was not due till nine. So he decided to take his bath at night instead of waiting till morning. Was he not sticky, and was not Paula coming to talk to him? He was delighted the thought had occurred to him. As he soused his head in the trough, he wondered what the little creatures that lived in the velvety silt at the bottom would think of the taste of soap. Laughing to himself, he squeezed his cloth into the water. He washed himself from head to foot, standing in the fresh, forsaken corner of the field, where no one could see him by daylight, so that now, in the veiled grey tinge of moonlight, he was no more noticeable than the crowded flowers. The night had on a new look: he never remembered to have seen the lustrous grey sheen of it before, nor to have noticed how vital the lights looked, like live folk inhabiting the silvery spaces. And the tall trees, wrapped obscurely in their mantles, would not have surprised him had they begun to move in converse. As he dried himself, he discovered little wanderings in the air, felt on his sides soft touches and caresses that were peculiarly delicious: sometimes they startled him, and he laughed as if he were not alone. The flowers, the meadow-sweet particularly, haunted him. He reached to put his hand over their fleeciness. They touched his thighs. Laughing, he gathered them and dusted himself all over with their cream dust and fragrance. For a moment he hesitated in wonder at himself: but the subtle glow in the hoary and black night reassured him. Things never had looked so personal and full of beauty, he had never known the wonder in himself before.

At nine o'clock he was waiting under the elder bush, in a state of high trepidation, but feeling that he was worthy, having a sense of his own wonder. She was late. At a quarter-past nine she came, flitting swiftly, in her own eager way.

'No, she would *not* go to sleep,' said Paula, with a world of wrath in her tone. He laughed bashfully. They wandered out into the dim, hill-side field.

'I have sat – in that bedroom – for an hour, for hours,' she cried indignantly. She took a deep breath: 'Ah, breathe!' she smiled.

She was very intense, and full of energy.

'I want' – she was clumsy with the language – 'I want – I should laike – to run – there!' She pointed across the field.

'Let's run, then,' he said curiously.

'Yes!'

And in an instant she was gone. He raced after her. For all he was so young and limber, he had difficulty in catching her. At first he could scarcely see her, though he could hear the rustle of her dress. She sped with astonishing fleetness. He overtook her, caught her by the arm, and they stood panting, facing one another with laughter.

'I could win,' she asserted blithely.

'Tha couldna,' he replied, with a peculiar, excited laugh.

28

They walked on, rather breathless. In front of them suddenly appeared the dark shapes of the three feeding horses.

'We ride a horse?' she said.

'What, bareback?' he asked.

'You say?' She did not understand.

'With no saddle?'

'No saddle – yes – no saddle.'

'Coop, lass!' he said to the mare, and in a minute he had her by the forelock, and was leading her down to the stacks, where he put a halter on her. She was a big, strong mare. Maurice seated the Fräulein, clambered himself in front of the girl, using the wheel of the wagon as a mount, and together they trotted uphill, she holding lightly round his waist. From the crest of the hill they looked round.

The sky was darkening with an awning of cloud. On the left the hill rose black and wooded, made cosy by a few lights from cottages along the highway. The hill spread to the right, and tufts of trees shut round. But in front was a great vista of night, a sprinkle of cottage candles, a twinkling cluster of lights, like an elfish fair in full swing, at the colliery an encampment of light at a village, a red flare on the sky far off, above an iron-foundry, and in the farthest distance the dim breathing of town lights. As they watched the night stretch far out, her arms tightened round his waist, and he pressed his elbows to his side, pressing her arms closer still. The horse moved restlessly. They clung to each other.

'Tha daesna want to go right away?' he asked the girl behind him.

'I stay with you,' she answered softly, and he felt her crouching close against him. He laughed curiously. He was afraid to kiss her, though he was urged to do so. They remained still, on the restless horse, watching the small lights lead deep into the night, in infinite distance.

'I don't want to go,' he said, in a tone half pleading.

She did not answer. The horse stirred restlessly.

'Let him run,' cried Paula, 'fast!'

She broke the spell, startled him into a little fury. He kicked the mare, hit her, and away she plunged down-hill. The girl clung tightly to the young man. They were riding bareback down a rough, steep hill. Maurice clung hard with hands and knees. Paula held him fast round the waist, leaning her head on his shoulders, and thrilling with excitement.

'We shall be off, we shall be off,' he cried, laughing with excitement; but she only crouched behind and pressed tight to him. The mare tore across the field. Maurice expected every moment to be flung on to the grass. He gripped with all the strength of his knees. Paula tucked herself behind him, and often wrenched him almost from his hold. Man and girl were taut with effort.

At last the mare came to a standstill, blowing. Paula slid off, and in an instant Maurice was beside her. They were both highly excited. Before he knew what he was doing, he had her in his arms, fast, and was kissing her, and laughing. They did not move for some time. Then, in silence, they walked towards the stacks.

It had grown quite dark, the night was thick with cloud. He walked with his arm round Paula's waist, she with her arm round him. They were near the stacks when Maurice felt a spot of rain.

'It's going to rain,' he said.

'Rain!' she echoed, as if it were trivial.

'I s'll have to put the stack-cloth on,' he said gravely. She did not understand.

When they got to the stacks, he went round to the shed, to return staggering in the darkness under the burden of the immense and heavy cloth. It had not been used once during the hay harvest.

'What are you going to do?' asked Paula, coming close to him in the darkness.

'Cover the top of the stack with it,' he replied. 'Put it over the stack, to keep the rain out.'

'Ah!' she cried, 'up there!' He dropped his burden. 'Yes,' he answered.

Fumbling he reared the long ladder up the side of the stack. He could not see the top.

'I hope it's solid,' he said softly.

A few smart drops of rain sounded drumming on the cloth. They seemed like another presence. It was very dark indeed between the great buildings of hay. She looked up the black wall and shrank to him.

'You carry it up there?' she asked.

'Yes,' he answered.

'I help you?' she said.

And she did. They opened the cloth. He clambered first up the steep ladder, bearing the upper part, she followed closely, carrying her full share. They mounted the shaky ladder in silence, stealthily.

4

As they climbed the stacks a light stopped at the gate on the high road. It was Geoffrey, come to help his brother with the cloth. Afraid of his own intrusion, he wheeled his bicycle silently towards the shed. This was a corrugated iron erection, on the opposite side of the hedge from the stacks. Geoffrey let his light go in front of him, but there was no sign from the lovers. He thought he saw a shadow slinking away. The light of the bicycle lamp sheered yellowly across the dark, catching a glint of raindrops, a mist of darkness, shadow of leaves, and strokes of long grass. Geoffrey entered the shed – no one was there. He walked slowly and doggedly round to the stacks. He had passed the wagon, when he heard something sheering down upon him. Starting back under the wall of hay, he saw the long ladder slither across the side of the stack, and fall with a bruising ring.

'What wor that?' he heard Maurice, aloft, ask cautiously.

'Something fall,' came the curious, almost pleased voice of the Fräulein.

'It wor niver th' ladder,' said Maurice. He peered over the side of the stack. He lay down, looking.

'It is an' a'l' he exclaimed. 'We knocked it down with the cloth, dragging it over.'

'We fast up here?' she exclaimed with a thrill.

'We are that – without I shout and make 'em hear at the Vicarage.'

'Oh no,' she said quickly.

'I don't want to,' he replied, with a short laugh. There came a swift clatter of raindrops on the cloth. Geoffrey crouched under the wall of the other stack.

'Mind where you tread – here, let me straighten this end,' said Maurice, with a peculiar intimate tone – a command and an embrace. 'We s'll have to sit under it. At any rate, we shan't get wet.'

'Not get wet!' echoed the girl, pleased, but agitated.

Geoffrey heard the slide and rustle of the cloth over the top of the stack, heard Maurice telling her to 'Mind!'

'Mind!' she repeated. 'Mind! you say "Mind!"'

'Well, what if I do?' he laughed. 'I don't want you to fall over th' side, do I?' His tone was masterful, but he was not quite sure of himself.

There was silence a moment or two.

'Maurice!' she said plaintively.

'I'm here,' he answered tenderly, his voice shaky with excitement that was near to distress. 'There, I've done. Now should we – we'll sit under this corner.'

'Maurice!' she was rather pitiful.

'What? You'll be all right,' he remonstrated, tenderly indignant.

'I be all raïght,' she repeated, 'I be all raïght, Maurice?'

'Tha knows tha will – I canna ca' thee Powla. Should I ca' thee, Minnie?'

It was the name of a dead sister.

'Minnie?' she exclaimed in surprise.

'Aye, should I?'

She answered in full-throated German. He laughed shakily.

'Come on – come on under. But do yer wish you was safe in th' Vicarage? Should I shout for somebody?' he asked.

'I don't wish, no!' She was vehement.

'Art sure?' he insisted, almost indignantly.

'Sure – I quite sure.' She laughed.

Geoffrey turned away at the last words. Then the rain beat heavily. The lonely brother slouched miserably to the hut, where the rain played a mad tattoo. He felt very miserable, and jealous of Maurice.

His bicycle lamp, downcast, shone a yellow light on the stark floor of the shed or hut with one wall open. It lit up the trodden earth, the shafts of tools lying piled under the beam, beside the dreary grey metal of the building. He took off the lamp, shone it round the hut. There were piles of harness, tools, a big sugar-box, a deep bed of hay – then the beams across the corrugated iron, all very dreary and stark. He shone the lamp into the night: nothing but the furtive glitter of raindrops through the mist of darkness, and black shapes hovering round.

Geoffrey blew out the light and flung himself on to the hay. He would put the ladder up for them in a while, when they would be wanting it. Meanwhile he sat and gloated over Maurice's felicity. He was imaginative, and now he had something concrete to work upon. Nothing in the whole of life stirred him so profoundly, and so utterly, as the thought of this woman. For Paula was strange, foreign, different from the ordinary girls: the rousing, feminine quality seemed in her concentrated, brighter, more fascinating than in anyone he had known, so that he felt most like a moth near a candle. He would have loved her wildly – but Maurice had got her. His thoughts beat the same course, round and round. What was it like when you kissed her, when she held you tight round the waist, how did she feel towards Maurice, did she love to touch him, was he fine and attractive to her; what did she think of himself – she merely disregarded him, as she would disregard a horse in a field; why would she do so, why couldn't he make her regard himself, instead of Maurice: he would never command a woman's regard like that, he always gave in to her too soon; if only some woman would come and take him for what he was worth, though he was such a stumbler and showed to such disadvantage, ah, what a grand thing it would be; how he would kiss her. Then round he went again in the same course, brooding almost like a madman. Meanwhile the rain drummed

33

deep on the shed, then grew lighter and softer. There came the drip, drip of the drops falling outside.

Geoffrey's heart leaped up his chest, and he clenched himself, as a black shape crept round the post of the shed and, bowing, entered silently. The young man's heart beat so heavily in plunges, he could not get his breath to speak. It was shock, rather than fear. The form felt towards him. He sprang up, gripped it with his great hand's panting 'Now, then!'

There was no resistance, only a little whimper of despair.

'Let me go,' said a woman's voice.

'What are you after?' he asked, in deep, gruff tones.

'I thought 'e was 'ere,' she wept despairingly, with little, stubborn sobs.

'An' you've found what you didn't expect, have you?'

At the sound of his bullying she tried to get away from him.

'Let me go,' she said.

'Who did you expect to find here?' he asked, but more his natural self.

'I expected my husband – him as you saw at dinner. Let me go.'

'Why, is it you?' exclaimed Geoffrey. 'Has he left you?'

'Let me go,' said the women sullenly, trying to draw away. He realized that the sleeve was very wet, her arm slender under his grasp. Suddenly he grew ashamed of himself: he had no doubt hurt her, gripping her so hard. He relaxed, but did not let her go.

'An' are you searching round after that snipe as was here at dinner?' he asked. She did not answer.

'Where did he leave you?'

'I left him – here. I've seen nothing of him since.'

'I s'd think it's good riddance,' he said. She did not answer. He gave a short laugh, saying:

'I should ha' thought you wouldn't ha' wanted to clap eyes on him again.'

'He's my husband – an' he's not go n' to run off if I can stop him.'

Geoffrey was silent, not knowing what to say.

'Have you got a jacket on?' he asked at last.

'What do you think? You've got hold of it.'

'You're wet through, aren't you?'

'I shouldn't be dry, comin' through that teemin' rain. But 'e's not here, so I'll go.'

'I mean,' he said humbly, 'are you wet through?'

She did not answer. He felt her shiver.

'Are you cold?' he asked, in surprise and concern.

She did not answer. He did not know what to say.

'Stop a minute,' he said, and he fumbled in his pocket for his matches. He struck a light, holding it in the hollow of his large, hard palm. He was a big man, and he looked anxious. Shedding the light on her, he saw she was rather pale, and very weary looking. Her old sailor hat was sodden and drooping with rain. She wore a fawn-coloured jacket of smooth cloth. This jacket was black-wet where the rain had beaten, her skirt hung sodden, and dripped on to her boots. The match went out.

'Why, you're wet through!' he said.

She did not answer.

'Shall you stop in here while it gives over?' he asked. She did not answer.

''Cause if you will, you'd better take your things off, an' have th' rug. There's a horse-rug in the box.'

He waited, but she would not answer. So he lit his bicycle lamp, and rummaged in the box, pulling out a large brown blanket, striped with scarlet and yellow. She stood stock still. He shone the light on her. She was very pale, and trembling fitfully.

'Are you that cold?' he asked in concern. 'Take your jacket off, and your hat, and put this right over you.'

Mechanically, she undid the enormous fawn-coloured buttons, and unpinned her hat. With her black hair drawn back from her low, honest brow, she looked little more than a girl, like a girl driven hard with womanhood by stress of life. She was small, and natty, with neat little features. But she shivered convulsively.

'Is something a-matter with you?' he asked.

'I've walked to Bulwell and back,' she quivered, 'looking

35

for him – an' I've not touched a thing since this morning.' She did not weep – she was too dreary-hardened to cry. He looked at her in dismay, his mouth half open: 'Gormin' as Maurice would have said.

''Aven't you had nothing to eat?' he said.

Then he turned aside to the box. There, the bread remaining was kept, and the great piece of cheese, and such things as sugar and salt, with all table utensils: there was some butter.

She sat down drearily on the bed of hay. He cut her a piece of bread and butter, and a piece of cheese. This she took, but ate listlessly.

'I want a drink,' she said.

'We 'aven't got no beer,' he answered. 'My father doesn't have it.'

'I want water,' she said.

He took a can and plunged through the wet darkness, under the great black hedge, down to the trough. As he came back he saw her in the half-lit little cave sitting bunched together. The soaked grass wet his feet – he thought of her. When he gave her a cup of water, her hand touched his and he felt her fingers hot and glossy. She trembled so she spilled the water.

'Do you feel badly?' he asked.

'I can't keep myself still – but it's only with being tired and having nothing to eat.'

He scratched his head contemplatively, waited while she ate her piece of bread and butter. Then he offered her another piece.

'I don't want it just now,' she said.

'You'll have to eat summat,' he said.

'I couldn't eat any more just now.'

He put the piece down undecidedly on the box. Then there was another long pause. He stood up with bent head. The bicycle, like a restful animal, glittered behind him, turning towards the wall. The woman sat hunched on the hay, shivering.

'Can't you get warm?' he asked.

'I shall by an' by – don't you bother. I'm taking your seat – are you stopping here all night?'

36

'Yes.'

'I'll be goin' in a bit,' she said.

'Nay, I non want you to go. I'm thinkin' how you could get warm.'

'Don't you bother about me,' she remonstrated, almost irritably.

'I just want to see as the stacks is all right. You take your shoes an' stockin's an' all your wet things off: you can easy wrap yourself all over in that rug, there's not so much of you.'

'It's raining – I s'll be all right – I s'll be going in a minute.'

'I've got to see as the stacks is safe. Take your wet things off.'

'Are you coming back?' she asked.

'I mightn't, not till morning.'

'Well, I s'll be gone in ten minutes, then. I've no rights to be here, an I s'll not let anybody be turned out for me.'

'You won't be turning me out.'

'Whether or no, I shan't stop.'

'Well, shall you if I come back?' he asked. She did not answer.

He went. In a few moments, she blew the light out. The rain was falling steadily, and the night was a black gulf. All was intensely still. Geoffrey listened everywhere: no sound save the rain. He stood between the stacks, but only heard the trickle of water, and the light swish of rain. Everything was lost in blackness. He imagined death was like that, many things dissolved in silence and darkness, blotted out, but existing. In the dense blackness he felt himself almost extinguished. He was afraid he might not find things the same. Almost frantically, he stumbled, feeling his way, till his hand touched the wet metal. He had been looking for a gleam of light.

'Did you blow the lamp out?' he asked, fearful lest the silence should answer him.

'Yes,' she answered humbly. He was glad to hear her voice. Groping into the pitch-dark shed, he knocked against the box, part of whose cover served as table. There was a clatter and a fall.

'That's the lamp, an' the knife, an' the cup,' he said. He struck a match.

'Th' cup's not broke.' He put it into the box.

'But th' oil's spilled out o' th' lamp. It always was a rotten old thing.' He hastily blew out his match, which was burning his fingers. Then he struck another light.

'You don't want a lamp, you know you don't, and I s'll be going directly, so you come an' lie down an' get your night's rest. I'm not taking any of your place.'

He looked at her by the light of another match. She was a queer little bundle, all brown, with gaudy border folding in and out, and her little face peering at him. As the match went out she saw him beginning to smile.

'I can sit right at this end,' she said. 'You lie down.'

He came and sat on the hay, at some distance from her. After a spell of silence:

'Is he really your husband?' he asked.

'He is!' she answered grimly.

'Hm!' Then there was silence again.

After a while: 'Are you warm now?'

'Why do you bother yourself?'

'I don't bother myself – do you follow him because you like him?' He put it very timidly. He wanted to know.

'I don't – I wish he was dead,' this with bitter contempt. Then doggedly: 'But he's my husband.'

He gave a short laugh.

'By Gad!' he said.

Again, after a while: 'Have you been married long?'

'Four years.'

'Four years – why, how old are you?'

'Twenty-three.'

'Are you turned twenty-three?'

'Last May.'

'Then you're four month older than me.' He mused over it. They were only two voices in the pitch-black night. It was eerie silence again.

'And do you just tramp about?' he asked.

'He reckons he's looking for a job. But he doesn't like work

38

in any shape or form. He was a stableman when I married him, at Greenhalgh's, the horse-dealers, at Chesterfield, where I was housemaid. He left that job when the baby was only two months, and I've been badgered about from pillar to post ever sin'. They say a rolling stone gathers no moss ...'

'An' where's the baby?'

'It died when it was ten months old.'

Now the silence was clinched between them. It was quite a long time before Geoffrey ventured to say sympathetically: 'You haven't much to look forward to.'

'I've wished many a score time when I've started shiverin' an' shakin' at nights, as I was taken bad for death. But we're not that handy at dying.'

He was silent. 'But whatever shall you do?' he faltered.

'I s'll find him, if I drop by th' road.'

'Why?', he asked, wondering, looking her way, though he saw nothing but solid darkness.

'Because I shall. He's not going to have it all his own road.'

'But why don't you leave him?'

'Because he's *not goin' to have it all his own road.*'

She sounded very determined, even vindictive. He sat in wonder, feeling uneasy, and vaguely miserable on her behalf. She sat extraordinarily still. She seemed like a voice only, a presence.

'Are you warm now?' he asked, half afraid.

'A bit warmer – but my feet!' She sounded pitiful.

'Let me warm them with my hands,' he asked her. 'I'm hot enough.'

'No, thank you,' she said coldly.

Then, in the darkness, she felt she had wounded him. He was writhing under her rebuff, for his offer had been pure kindness.

'They're 'appen dirty,' she said, half mocking.

'Well – mine is – an' I have a bath a'most every day,' he answered.

'I don't know when they'll get warm,' she moaned to herself.

'Well, then, put them in my hands.'

39

She heard him faintly rattling the match-box, and then a phosphorescent glare began to fume in his direction. Presently he was holding two smoking, blue-green blotches of light towards her feet. She was afraid. But her feet ached so, and the impulse drove her on, so she placed her soles lightly on the two blotches of smoke. His large hands clasped over her instep, warm and hard.

'They're like ice!' he said, in deep concern.

He warmed her feet as best he could, putting them close against him. Now and again convulsive tremors ran over her. She felt his warm breath on the balls of her toes, that were bunched up in his hands. Leaning forward, she touched his hair delicately with her fingers. He thrilled. She fell to gently stroking his hair, with timid, pleading finger-tips.

'Do they feel any better?' he asked, in a low voice, suddenly lifting his face to her. This sent her hand sliding softly over his face, and her finger-tips caught on his mouth. She drew quickly away. He put his hand out to find hers, in his other palm holding both her feet. His wandering hand met her face. He touched it curiously. It was wet. He put his big fingers cautiously on her eyes, into two little pools of tears.

'What's a matter?' he asked in a low, choked voice.

She leaned down to him and gripped him tightly round the neck, pressing him to her bosom in a little frenzy of pain. Her bitter disillusionment with life, her unalleviated shame and degradation during the last four years, had driven her into loneliness, and hardened her till a large part of her nature was caked and sterile. Now she softened again, and her spring might be beautiful. She had been in a fair way to make an ugly old woman.

She clasped the head of Geoffrey to her breast, which heaved and fell, and heaved again. He was bewildered, full of wonder. He allowed the woman to do as she would with him. Her tears fell on his hair, as she wept noiselessly; and he breathed deep as she did. At last she let go her clasp. He put his arms round her.

'Come and let me warm you,' he said, folding up on his knee and lapping her with his heavy arms against himself. She was small and *câline*. He held her very warm and close. Presently she stole her arms round him.

'You *are* big,' she whispered.

He gripped her hard, started, put his mouth down wanderingly, seeking her out. His lips met her temple. She slowly, deliberately turned her mouth to his, and with opened lips, met him in a kiss, his first love kiss.

5

It was breaking cold dawn when Geoffrey woke. The woman was still sleeping in his arms. Her face in sleep moved all his tenderness: the tight shutting of her mouth, as if in resolution to bear what was very hard to bear, contrasted so pitifully with the small mould of her features. Geoffrey pressed her to his bosom: having her, he felt he could bruise the lips of the scornful, and pass on erect, unabateable. With her to complete him, to form the core of him, he was firm and whole. Needing her so much, he loved her fervently.

Meanwhile the dawn came like death, one of those slow, livid mornings that seem to come in a cold sweat. Slowly, and painfully, the air began to whiten. Geoffrey saw it was not raining. As he was watching the ghastly transformation outside, he felt aware of something. He glanced down: she was open-eyed, watching him; she had golden-brown, calm eyes, that immediately smiled into his. He also smiled, bowed softly down and kissed her. They did not speak for some time. Then:

'What's thy name?' he asked curiously.

'Lydia,' she said.

'Lydia!' he repeated wonderingly. He felt rather shy.

'Mine's Geoffrey Wookey,' he said.

She merely smiled at him.

They were silent for a considerate time. By morning light, things look small. The huge trees of the evening were dwindled to hoary, small, uncertain things, trespassing in the sick pallor of the atmosphere. There was a dense mist, so that the light could scarcely breathe. Everything seemed to quiver with cold and sickliness.

'Have you often slept out?' he asked her.

'Not so very,' she answered.

'You won't go after *him*?' he asked.

'I s'll have to,' she replied, but she nestled in to Geoffrey. He felt a sudden panic.

'You mustn't,' he exclaimed, and she saw he was afraid for himself. She let it be, was silent.

'We couldn't get married?' he asked thoughtfully.

'No.'

He brooded deeply over this. At length:

'Would you go to Canada with me?'

'We'll see what you think in two months' time,' she replied quietly, without bitterness.

'I s'll think the same,' he protested, hurt.

She did not answer, only watched him steadily. She was there for him to do as he liked with; but she would not injure his fortunes; no, not to save his soul.

'Haven't you got no relations?' he asked.

'A married sister at Crick.'

'On a farm?'

'No – married a farm labourer – but she's very comfortable. I'll go there, if you want me to, just till I can get another place in service.'

He considered this.

'Could you get on a farm?' he asked wistfully.

'Greenhalgh's was a farm.'

He saw the future brighten: she would be a help to him. She agreed to go to her sister, and to get a place of service – until spring, he said, when they would sail for Canada. He waited for the assent.

'You will come with me, then?' he asked.

'When the time comes,' she said.

Her want of faith made him bow his head: she had reason for it.

'Shall you walk to Crick, or go from Langley Mill to Ambergate? But it's only ten mile to walk. So we can go together up Hunt's Hill – you'd have to go past our lane-end, then I could easy nip down an' fetch you some money,' he said humbly.

'I've got half a sovereign by me – it's more than I s'll want.'

'Let's see it,' he said.

After a while, fumbling under the blanket, she brought out the piece of money. He felt she was independent of him. Brooding rather bitterly, he told himself she'd forsake him. His anger gave him courage to ask:

'Shall you go in service in your maiden name?'

'No.'

He was bitterly wrathful with her – full of resentment.

'I bet I s'll niver see you again,' he said, with a short, hard laugh. She put her arms round him, pressed him to her bosom, while the tears rose to her eyes. He was reassured, but not satisfied.

'Shall you write to me tonight?'

'Yes, I will.'

'And can I write to you – who shall I write to?'

'Mrs Bredon.'

'"Bredon"!' he repeated bitterly.

He was exceedingly uneasy.

The dawn had grown quite wan. He saw the hedges drooping wet down the grey mist. Then he told her about Maurice.

'Oh, you *shouldn't*!' she said. 'You should ha' put the ladder up for them, you *should*.'

'Well – I don't care.'

'Go and do it now – and I'll go.'

'No, don't you. Stop an' see our Maurice; go on, stop an' see him – then I'll be able to tell him.'

She consented in silence. He had her promise she would not go before he returned. She adjusted her dress, found her way to the trough, where she performed her toilet.

Geoffrey wandered round to the upper field. The stacks looked wet in the mist, the hedge was drenched. Mist rose like steam from the grass, and the near hills were veiled almost to a shadow. In the valley, some peaks of black poplar showed fairly definite, jutting up. He shivered with chill.

There was no sound from the stacks, and he could see nothing. After all, he wondered, were they up there? But he reared the ladder to the place whence it had been swept, then went down the hedge to gather dry sticks. He was breaking off thin dead twigs under a holly tree when he heard, on the perfectly still air: 'Well, I'm dashed!'

He listened intently. Maurice was awake.

'Sithee here!' the lad's voice exclaimed. Then, after a while, the foreign sound of the girl:

'What – oh, thair!'

'Aye, th' ladder's there, right enough.'

'You said it had fall down.'

'Well, I heard it drop – an' I couldna feel it nor see it.'

'You said it had fall down – you lie, you liar.'

'Nay, as true as I'm here –'

'You tell me lies – make me stay here – you tell me lies –' She was passionately indignant.

'As true as I'm standing here –' he began.

'Lies! – lies! – lies!' she cried. 'I don't believe you, never. You *mean*, you *mean, mean, mean!*'

'A' raïght, then!' He was now incensed, in his turn.

'You are bad, mean, mean, mean.'

'Are ter commin' down?' asked Maurice coldly.

'No – I will not come with you – mean, to tell me lies.'

'Are ter commin' down?'

'No, I don't want you.'

'A' raïght, then!'

Geoffrey, peering through the holly tree, saw Maurice negotiating the ladder. The top rung was below the brim of the stack, and rested on the cloth, so it was dangerous to approach. The Fräulein watched him from the end of the stack, where the cloth thrown back showed the light, dry hay. He slipped slightly, she screamed. When he had got on to the ladder, he pulled the cloth away, throwing it back, making it easy for her to descend.

'Now are ter commin'?' he asked.

'No!' She shook her head violently, in a pet.

Geoffrey felt slightly contemptuous of her. But Maurice waited.

'Are ter commin'?' he called again.

'No,' she flashed, like a wild cat.

'All right, then I'm going.'

He descended. At the bottom, he stood holding the ladder.

'Come on, while I hold it steady,' he said.

There was no reply. For some minutes he stood patiently with his foot on the bottom rung of the ladder. He was pale, rather washed-out in his appearance, and he drew himself together with cold.

'Are ter commin', or aren't ter?' he asked at length. Still there was no reply.

'Then stop up till tha'rt ready,' he muttered, and he went away. Round the other side of the stacks he met Geoffrey.

'What, are thaïgh here?' he exclaimed.

'Bin here a' naïght,' replied Geoffrey. 'I come to help thee wi' th' cloth, but I found it on, an' th' ladder down, so I thowt tha'd gone.'

'Did ter put th' ladder up?'

'I did a bit sin'.'

Maurice brooded over this, Geoffrey struggled with himself to get out his own news. At last he blurted:

'Tha knows that woman as wor here yis'day dinner – 'er come back, an' stopped i' th' shed a' night, out o' th' rain.'

'Oh – ah!' said Maurice, his eye kindling, and a smile crossing his pallor.

'An' I s'll gi'e her some breakfast.'

'Oh – ah!' repeated Maurice.

'It's th' man as is good-for-nowt, not her,' protested Geoffrey. Maurice did not feel in a position to cast stones.

'Tha pleases thysen,' he said, 'what ter does.' He was very quiet, unlike himself. He seemed bothered and anxious, as Geoffrey had not seen him before.

'What's up wi' thee?' asked the elder brother, who in his own heart was glad, and relieved.

'Nowt,' was the reply.

They went together to the hut. The woman was folding the blanket. She was fresh from washing, and looked very pretty. Her hair, instead of being screwed tightly back, was coiled in a knot low down, partly covering her ears. Before she had deliberately made herself plain-looking: now she was neat and pretty, with a sweet, womanly gravity.

'Hello. I didn't think to find you here,' said Maurice, very awkwardly, smiling. She watched him gravely without reply. 'But it was better in shelter than outside last night,' he added.

'Yes,' she replied.

'Shall you get a few more sticks?' Geoffrey asked him. It was a new thing for Geoffrey to be leader. Maurice obeyed. He wandered forth into the damp, raw morning. He did not go to the stack, as he shrank from meeting Paula.

At the mouth of the hut, Geoffrey was making the fire. The woman got out coffee from the box: Geoffrey set the tin to boil. They were arranging breakfast when Paula appeared. She was hatless. Bits of hay stuck in her hair, and she was white-faced – altogether, she did not show to advantage.

'Ah – you!' she exclaimed, seeing Geoffrey.

'Hello!' he answered. 'You're out early.'

'Where's Maurice?'

'I dunno, he should be back directly.'

Paula was silent.

'When have you come?' she asked.

'I come last night, but I could see nobody about. I got up half an hour sin', an' put th' ladder up ready to take the stack-cloth up.'

Paula understood, and was silent. When Maurice returned with the faggots, she was crouched warming her hands. She looked up at him, but he kept his eyes averted from her. Geoffrey met the eyes of Lydia, and smiled. Maurice put his hands to the fire.

'You cold?' asked Paula tenderly.

'A bit,' he answered, quite friendly, but reserved. And all the while the four sat round the fire, drinking their smoked coffee, eating each a small piece of toasted bacon, Paula watched eagerly for the eyes of Maurice, and he avoided her.

46

He was gentle, but would not give his eyes to her looks. And Geoffrey smiled constantly to Lydia, who watched gravely.

The German girl succeeded in getting safely into the Vicarage, her escapade unknown to anyone save the housemaid. Before a week was out, she was openly engaged to Maurice, and when her month's notice expired, she went to live at the farm.

Geoffrey and Lydia kept faith one with the other.

The Lovely Lady

At seventy-two, Pauline Attenborough could still sometimes be mistaken, in the half-light, for thirty. She really was a wonderfully preserved woman, of perfect *chic*. Of course, it helps a great deal to have the right frame. She would be an exquisite skeleton, and her skull would be an exquisite skull, like that of some Etruscan woman, with feminine charm still in the swerve of the bone and the pretty naïve teeth.

Mrs Attenborough's face was of the perfect oval, and slightly flat type that wears best. There is no flesh to sag. Her nose rode serenely, in its finely bridged curve. Only her big grey eyes were a tiny bit prominent on the surface of her face, and they gave her away most. The bluish lids were heavy, as if they ached sometimes with the strain of keeping the eyes beneath them arch and bright; and at the corners of the eyes were fine little wrinkles which would slacken with haggardness, then be pulled up tense again, to that bright, gay look like a Leonardo woman who really could laugh outright.

Her niece Cecilia was perhaps the only person in the world who was aware of the invisible little wire which connected Pauline's eye-wrinkles with Pauline's will-power. Only Cecilia *consciously* watched the eyes go haggard and old and tired, and remain so, for hours; until Robert came home. Then ping! – the mysterious little wire that worked between Pauline's will and her face went taut, the weary, haggard, prominent eyes suddenly began to gleam, the eyelids arched, the queer curved eyebrows which floated in such frail arches on Pauline's forehead began to gather a mocking significance, and you had the *real* lovely lady, in all her charm.

She really had the secret of everlasting youth; that is to say, she could don her youth again like an eagle. But she was sparing of it. She was wise enough not to try being young for too many people. Her son Robert, in the evenings, and Sir Wilfred Knipe sometimes in the afternoon to tea: then

49

occasional visitors on Sunday, when Robert was home: for
these she was her lovely and changeless self, that age could
not wither, nor custom stale: so bright and kindly and yet
subtly mocking, like Mona Lisa, who knew a thing or two.
But Pauline knew more, so she needn't be smug at all, she
could laugh that lovely mocking Bacchante laugh of hers,
which was at the same time never malicious, always good-
naturedly tolerant, both of virtues and vices. The former,
of course, taking much more tolerating. So she suggested,
roguishly.

Only with her niece Cecilia she did not trouble to keep up
the glamour. Ciss was not very observant, anyhow: and
more than that, she was plain: more still, she was in love
with Robert: and most of all, she was thirty, and dependent
on her Aunt Pauline. Oh, Cecilia! Why make music for
her!

Cecilia, called by her aunt and by her cousin Robert just
Ciss, like a cat spitting, was a big dark-complexioned, pug-
faced young woman who very rarely spoke, and when she
did, couldn't get it out. She was the daughter of a poor Con-
gregational minister who had been, while he lived, brother
to Ronald, Aunt Pauline's husband. Ronald and the Con-
gregational minister were both well dead, and Aunt Pauline
had had charge of Ciss for the last five years.

They lived all together in a quite exquisite though rather
small Queen Anne house some twenty-five miles out of town,
secluded in a little dale, and surrounded by small but very
quaint and pleasant grounds. It was an ideal place and an
ideal life for Aunt Pauline, at the age of seventy-two. When
the kingfishers flashed up the little stream in the garden,
going under the alders, something still flashed in her heart.
She was that kind of woman.

Robert, who was two years older than Ciss, went every
day to town, to his chambers in one of the Inns. He was a
barrister, and, to his secret but very deep mortification, he
earned about a hundred pounds a year. He simply *couldn't*
get above that figure, though it was rather easy to get below
it. Of course, it didn't matter. Pauline had money. But then

what was Pauline's was Pauline's, and though she could give
almost lavishly, still, one was always aware of having a *lovely*
and *undeserved* present made to one: presents are so much
nicer when they are undeserved, Aunt Pauline would say.

Robert too was plain, and almost speechless. He was
medium-sized, rather broad and stout, though not fat. Only
his creamy, clean-shaven face was rather fat, and sometimes
suggestive of an Italian priest, in its silence and its secrecy.
But he had grey eyes like his mother, but very shy and
uneasy, not bold like hers. Perhaps Ciss was the only person
who fathomed his awful shyness and *malaise*, his habitual
feeling that he was in the wrong place: almost like a soul
that has got into the wrong body. But he never did anything about it. He went up to his chambers and read law.
It was, however, all the weird old processes that interested
him. He had, unknown to everybody but his mother, a quite
extraordinary collection of old Mexican legal documents, re-
ports of processes and trials, pleas, accusations, the weird
and awful mixture of ecclesiastical law and common law in
seventeenth-century Mexico. He had started a study in this
direction through coming across a report of a trial of two
English sailors, for murder, in Mexico in 1620, and he had
gone on, when the next document was an accusation against
a Don Miguel Estrada for seducing one of the nuns of the
Sacred Heart Convent in Oaxaca in 1680.

Pauline and her son Robert had wonderful evenings with
these old papers. The lovely lady knew a little Spanish. She
even looked a trifle Spanish herself, with a high comb and a
marvellous dark brown shawl embroidered in thick silvery
silk embroidery. So she would sit at the perfect old table,
soft as velvet in its deep brown surface, a high comb in her
hair, ear-rings with dropping pendants in her ears, her arms
bare and still beautiful, a few strings of pearls round her
throat, a puce velvet dress on and this or another beautiful
shawl, and by candle-light she looked, yes, a Spanish high-
bred beauty of thirty-two or three. She set the candles to
give her face just the chiaroscuro she knew suited her; her
high chair that rose behind her face was done in old green

brocade, against which her face emerged like a Christmas rose.

They were always three at table; and they always drank a bottle of champagne: Pauline two glasses, Ciss two glasses, Robert the rest. The lovely lady sparkled and was radiant. Ciss, her black hair bobbed, her broad shoulders in a very nice and becoming dress that Aunt Pauline had helped her to make, stared from her aunt to her cousin and back again, with rather confused, mute, hazel eyes, and played the part of an audience suitably impressed. She *was* impressed, somewhere, all the time And even rendered speechless by Pauline's brilliancy, even after five years. But at the bottom of her consciousness were the data of as weird a document as Robert ever studied: all the things she knew about her aunt and cousin.

Robert was always a gentleman, with an old-fashioned punctilious courtesy that covered his shyness quite completely. He was, and Ciss knew it, more confused than shy. He was worse than she was. Cecilia's own confusion dated from only five years back – Robert's must have started before he was born. In the lovely lady's womb he must have felt *very* confused.

He paid all his attention to his mother, drawn to her as a humble flower to the sun. And yet, priest-like, he was all the time aware, with the tail of his consciousness, that Ciss was there, and that she was a bit shut out of it, and that something wasn't right. He was aware of the third consciousness in the room. Whereas to Pauline, her niece Cecilia was an appropriate part of her own setting, rather than a distinct consciousness.

Robert took coffee with his mother and Ciss in the warm drawing-room, where all the furniture was so lovely, all collectors' pieces – Mrs Attenborough had made her own money, dealing privately in pictures and furniture and rare things from barbaric countries – and the three talked desultorily till about eight or half past. It was very pleasant, very cosy, very homely even: Pauline made a real home cosiness out of so much elegant material. The chat was simple, and nearly always bright. Pauline was her *real* self, emanating a friendly mockery and an odd, ironic gaiety. Till there came a little pause.

At which Ciss always rose and said good night and carried out the coffee-tray, to prevent Burnett from intruding any more.

And then! Oh, then, the lovely glowing intimacy of the evening, between mother and son, when they deciphered manuscripts and discussed points, Pauline with that eagerness of a girl, for which she was famous. And it was quite genuine. In some mysterious way she had *saved up* her power for being thrilled, in connexion with a man. Robert, solid, rather quiet and subdued, seemed like the elder of the two: almost like a priest with a young girl pupil. And that was rather how he felt.

Ciss had a flat for herself just across the courtyard, over the old coach-house and stables. There were no horses. Robert kept his car in the coach-house. Ciss had three very nice rooms up there, stretching along in a row one after another, and she had got used to the ticking of the stable clock.

But sometimes she did not go up to her rooms. In the summer she would sit on the lawn, and from the open window of the drawing-room upstairs she would hear Pauline's wonderful heart-searching laugh. And in the winter the young woman would put on a thick coat and walk slowly to the little balustraded bridge over the stream, and then look back at the three lighted windows of that drawing-room where mother and son were so happy together.

Ciss loved Robert, and she believed that Pauline intended the two of them to marry: when she was dead. But poor Robert, he was so convulsed with shyness already, with man or woman. What would he be when his mother was dead – in a dozen more years? He would be just a shell, the shell of a man who had never lived.

The strange unspoken sympathy of the young with one another, when they are overshadowed by the old, was one of the bonds between Robert and Ciss. But another bond, which Ciss did not know how to draw tight, was the bond of passion. Poor Robert was by nature a passionate man. His silence and his agonized, though hidden, shyness were both the result of a secret physical passionateness. And how Pauline could play on this! Ah, Ciss was not blind to the eyes which he fixed on his mother, eyes fascinated yet humiliated, full of shame. He was ashamed that he was not a man. And he did not love his mother. He was fascinated by her. Completely fascinated. And for the rest, paralysed in a life-long confusion.

Ciss stayed in the garden till the lights leapt up in Pauline's bedroom – about ten o'clock. The lovely lady had retired. Robert would now stay another hour or so, alone. Then he too would retire. Ciss, in the dark outside, sometimes wished she could creep up to him and say: 'Oh, Robert! It's all wrong!' But Aunt Pauline would hear. And, anyhow, Ciss couldn't do it. She went off to her own rooms once more, and so for ever.

In the morning coffee was brought up on a tray to each of the three relatives. Ciss had to be at Sir Wilfred Knipe's at nine o'clock, to give two hours' lessons to his little grand-daughter. It was her sole serious occupation, except that she played the piano for the love of it. Robert set off to town about nine. And, as a rule, Aunt Pauline appeared at lunch, though sometimes not until tea-time. When she appeared, she looked fresh and young. But she was inclined to fade rather quickly, like a flower without water, in the day-time. Her hour was the candle hour.

So she always rested in the afternoon. When the sun shone, if possible she took a sun-bath. This was one of her secrets. Her lunch was very light, she could take her sun-and-air-bath before noon or after, as it pleased her. Often it was in the afternoon, when the sun shone very warmly into a queer little yew-walled square just behind the stables. Here Ciss stretched out the lying-chair and rugs, and put the light parasol in the silent little enclosure of thick dark yew hedges beyond the red walls of the unused stables. And hither came the lovely lady with her book. Ciss then had to be on guard in one of her own rooms, should her aunt, who was very keen-eared, hear a footstep.

One afternoon it occurred to Cecilia that she herself might

while away this rather long afternoon by taking a sun-bath. She was growing restive. The thought of the flat roof of the stable buildings, to which she could climb from a loft at the end, started her on a new adventure. She often went on to the roof: she had to, to wind up the stable clock, which was a job she had assumed to herself. Now she took a rug, climbed out under the heavens, looked at the sky and the great elm-tops, looked at the sun, then took off her things and lay down perfectly serenely, in a corner of the roof under the parapet, full in the sun.

It was rather lovely, to bask all one's length like this in warm sun and air. Yes, it was very lovely! It even seemed to melt some of the hard bitterness of her heart, some of that core of unspoken resentment which never dissolved. Luxuriously, she spread herself, so that the sun should touch her limbs fully, fully. If she had no other lover, she should have the sun! She rolled voluptuously. And suddenly her heart stood still in her body, and her hair almost rose on end as a voice said very softly, musingly in her ear:

'No, Henry dear! It was not my fault you died instead of marrying that Claudia. No, darling. I was quite, quite willing for you to marry her, unsuitable though she was.'

Cecilia sank down on her rug powerless and perspiring with dread. That awful voice, so soft, so musing, yet so unnatural. Not a human voice at all. Yet there must, there must be someone on the roof! Oh! how unspeakably awful!

She lifted her weak head and peeped across the sloping leads. Nobody! The chimneys were far too narrow to shelter anybody. There was nobody on the roof. Then it must be someone in the trees, in the elms. Either that, or terror unspeakable, a bodiless voice! She reared her head a little higher.

And as she did so, came the voice again:

'No, darling! I told you you would tire of her in six months. And you see, it was true, dear. It was true, true, true! I wanted to spare you that. So it wasn't I who made you feel weak and disabled, wanting that very silly Claudia; poor thing, she looked so woebegone afterwards! Wanting

her and not wanting her, you got *yourself* into that perplexity, my dear. I only warned you. What else could I do?
And you lost your spirit and died without ever knowing me
again. It was bitter, bitter –'

The voice faded away. Cecilia subsided weakly on to her
rug, after the anguished tension of listening. Oh, it was
awful. The sun shone, the sky was blue, all seemed so lovely
and afternoony and summery. And yet, oh, horror! – she was
going to be forced to believe in the supernatural! And she
loathed the supernatural, ghosts and voices and rappings and
all the rest.

But that awful creepy bodiless voice, with its rusty sort of
whisper of an overtone! It had something so fearfully
familiar in it too! and yet was so utterly uncanny. Poor
Cecilia could only lie there unclothed, and so all the more
agonizingly helpless, inert, collapsed in sheer dread.

And then she heard the thing sigh! A deep sigh that seemed
weirdly familiar, yet was not human. 'Ah, well; ah, well, the
heart must bleed! Better it should bleed than break. It is
grief, grief! But it wasn't my fault, dear. And Robert could
marry our poor dull Ciss tomorrow, if he wanted her. But
he doesn't care about it, so why force him into anything!'
The sounds were very uneven, sometimes only a husky sort
of whisper. Listen! Listen!

Cecilia was about to give vent to loud and piercing screams
of hysteria, when the last two sentences arrested her. All her
caution and her cunning sprang alert. It was Aunt Pauline!
It must be Aunt Pauline, practising ventriloquism or something like that! What a devil she was!

Where was she? She must be lying down there, right below
where Cecilia herself was lying. And it was either some
fiend's trick of ventriloquism, or else thought transference
that conveyed itself like sound. The sounds were very uneven. Sometimes quite inaudible, sometimes only a brushing sort of noise. Ciss listened intently. No, it could not be
ventriloquism. It was worse, some form of thought transference. Some horror of that sort. Cecilia still lay weak and
inert, terrified to move, but she was growing calmer with

suspicion. It was some diabolic trick of that unnatural woman.

But *what a devil* of a woman! She even knew that she, Cecilia, had mentally accused her of killing her son Henry. Poor Henry was Robert's elder brother, twelve years older than Robert. He had died suddenly when he was twenty-two, after an awful struggle with himself, because he was passionately in love with a young and very good-looking actress, and his mother had humorously despised him for the attachment. So he had caught some sudden ordinary disease, but the poison had gone to his brain and killed him before he ever regained consciousness. Ciss knew the few facts from her own father. And lately she had been thinking that Pauline was going to kill Robert as she had killed Henry. It was clear murder: a mother murdering her sensitive sons, who were fascinated by her: the Circe!

'I suppose I may as well get up,' murmured the dim, unbreaking voice. 'Too much sun is as bad as too little. Enough sun, enough love thrill, enough proper food, and not too much of any of them, and a woman might live for ever. I verily believe for ever. If she absorbs as much vitality as she expends! Or perhaps a trifle more!'

It was certainly Aunt Pauline! How, how horrible! She, Ciss, was hearing Aunt Pauline's thoughts. Oh, how ghastly! Aunt Pauline was sending out her thoughts in a sort of radio, and she, Ciss, had to *hear* what her aunt was thinking. How ghastly! How insufferable! One of them would surely have to die.

She twisted and she lay inert and crumpled, staring vacantly in front of her. Vacantly! Vacantly! And her eyes were staring almost into a hole. She was staring into it unseeing, a hole going down in the corner from the lead gutter. It meant nothing to her. Only it frightened her a little more.

When suddenly out of the hole came a sigh and a last whisper. 'Ah, well! Pauline! Get up, it's enough for to-day!' Good God! Out of the hole of the rain-pipe! The rain-pipe was acting as a speaking-tube! Impossible! No, quite possible. She had read of it even in some book. And Aunt Pauline, like the old and guilty woman she was, talked aloud to herself. That was it!

A sullen exultance sprang into Ciss's breast. *That* was why she would never have anybody, not even Robert, in her bedroom. That was why she never dozed in a chair, never sat absent-minded anywhere, but went to her room, and kept to her room, except when she roused herself to be alert. When she slackened off, she talked to herself! She talked in a soft little crazy voice to herself. But she was not crazy. It was only her thoughts murmuring themselves aloud.

So she had qualms about poor Henry! Well she might have! Ciss believed that Aunt Pauline had loved her big, handsome, brilliant first-born much more than she loved Robert, and that his death had been a terrible blow and a chagrin to her. Poor Robert had been only ten years old when Henry died. Since then he had been the substitute.

Ah, how awful!

But Aunt Pauline was a strange woman. She had left her husband when Henry was a small child, some years even before Robert was born. There was no quarrel. Sometimes she saw her husband again, quite amicably, but a little mockingly. And she even gave him money.

For Pauline earned all her own. Her father had been a consul in the East and in Naples: and a devoted collector of beautiful and exotic things. When he died, soon after his grandson Henry was born, he left his collection of treasures to his daughter. And Pauline, who had really a passion and a genius for loveliness, whether in texture or form or colour, had laid the basis of her fortune on her father's collection. She had gone on collecting, buying where she could, and selling to collectors and to museums. She was one of the first to sell old, weird African wooden figures to the museums, and ivory carvings from New Guinea. She bought Renoir as soon as she saw his pictures. But not Rousseau. And all by herself she made a fortune.

After her husband died, she had not married again. She was not even *known* to have had lovers. If she did have lovers, it was not among the men who admired her most and paid her devout and open attendance. To these she was a 'friend'.

Cecilia slipped on her clothes and caught up her rug, hastened carefully down the ladder to the loft. As she descended she heard the ringing musical call: 'All right, Ciss!' which meant that the lovely lady was finished, and returning to the house. Even her voice was marvellously young and sonorous, beautifully balanced and self-possessed. So different from the little voice in which she talked to herself. *That* was much more the voice of an old woman.

Ciss hastened round to the yew enclosure, where lay the comfortable chaise-longue with the various delicate rugs. Everything Pauline had was choice, to the fine straw mat on the floor. The great yew walls were beginning to cast long shadows. Only in the corner, where the rugs tumbled their delicate colours, was there hot, still sunshine.

The rugs folded up, the chair lifted away, Cecilia stooped to look at the mouth of the rain-pipe. There it was, in the corner, under a little hood of masonry and just projecting from the thick leaves of the creeper on the wall. If Pauline, lying there, turned her face towards the wall, she would speak into the very mouth of the hole. Cecilia was reassured. She had heard her aunt's thoughts indeed, but by no uncanny agency.

That evening, as if aware of something, Pauline was a little quicker than usual, though she looked her own serene, rather mysterious self. And after coffee she said to Robert and Ciss: 'I'm so sleepy. The sun has made me so sleepy. I feel full of sunshine like a bee. I shall go to bed, if you don't mind. You two sit and have a talk.'

Cecilia looked quickly at her cousin.

'Perhaps you would rather be alone,' she said to him.

'No, no,' he replied. 'Do keep me company for a while, if it doesn't bore you.'

The windows were open, the scent of the honeysuckle wafted in with the sound of an owl. Robert smoked in silence. There was a sort of despair in the motionless, rather squat body. He looked like a caryatid bearing a weight.

'Do you remember Cousin Henry?' Cecilia asked him suddenly.

He looked up in surprise.

'Yes, very well,' he said.

'What did he look like?' she said, glancing into her cousin's big, secret-troubled eyes, in which there was so much frustration.

'Oh, he was handsome: tall and fresh-coloured, with mother's soft brown hair.' As a matter of fact, Pauline's hair was grey. 'The ladies admired him very much; he was at all the dances.'

'And what kind of character had he?'

'Oh, very good-natured and jolly. He liked to be amused. He was rather quick and clever, like mother, and very good company.'

'And did he love your mother?'

'Very much. She loved him too – better than she does me, as a matter of fact. He was so much more nearly her idea of a man.'

'Why was he more her idea of a man?'

'Tall – handsome – attractive, and very good company – and would, I believe, have been very successful at law. I'm afraid I am merely negative in all those respects.'

Ciss looked at him attentively, with her slow-thinking hazel eyes. Under his impassive mask, she knew he suffered.

'Do you think you are so much more negative than he?' she said.

He did not lift his face. But after a few moments he replied:

'My life, certainly, is a negative affair.'

She hesitated before she dared ask him:

'And do you mind?'

He did not answer her at all. Her heart sank.

'You see, I am afraid my life is as negative as yours is,' she said. 'And I'm beginning to mind bitterly. I'm thirsty.'

She saw his creamy, well-bred hand tremble.

'I suppose,' he said, without looking at her, 'one will rebel when it is too late.'

That was queer, from him.

'Robert,' she said, 'do you like me at all?'

She saw his dusky, creamy face, so changeless in its folds, go pale. 'I am very fond of you,' he murmured.

'Won't you kiss me? Nobody ever kisses me,' she said pathetically.

He looked at her, his eyes strange with fear and a certain haughtiness. Then he rose and came softly over to her and kissed her gently on the cheek.

'It's an awful shame, Ciss!' he said softly.

She caught his hand and pressed it to her breast.

'And sit with me some time in the garden,' she said, murmuring with difficulty. 'Won't you?'

He looked at her anxiously and searchingly.

'What about mother?' he said.

Ciss smiled a funny little smile, and looked into his eyes. He suddenly flushed crimson, turning aside his face. It was a painful sight.

'I know,' he said, 'I am no lover of women.'

He spoke with sarcastic stoicism against himself, but even she did not know the shame it was to him.

'You never try to be!' she said.

Again his eyes changed uncannily.

'Does one have to try?' he said.

'Why, yes! One never does anything if one doesn't try.'

He went pale again.

'Perhaps you are right,' he said.

In a few minutes she left him and went to her room. At least, she had tried to take off the everlasting lid from things.

The weather continued sunny, Pauline continued her sun-baths, and Ciss lay on the roof eavesdropping in the literal sense of the word. But Pauline was not to be heard. No sound came up the pipe. She must be lying with her face away into the open. Ciss listened with all her might. She could just detect the faintest, faintest murmur away below, but no audible syllable.

And at night, under the stars, Cecilia sat and waited in silence, on the seat which kept in view the drawing-room windows and the side door into the garden. She saw the light go up in her aunt's room. She saw the lights at last go out in the drawing-room. And she waited. But he did not come. She stayed on in the darkness half the night, while the owl hooted. But she stayed alone.

Two days she heard nothing, her aunt's thoughts were not revealed and at evening nothing happened. Then the second night, as she sat with heavy, helpless persistence in the garden, suddenly she started. He had come out. She rose and went softly over the grass to him.

'Don't speak,' he murmured.

And in silence, in the dark, they walked down the garden and over the little bridge to the paddock, where the hay, cut very late, was in cock. There they stood disconsolate under the stars.

'You see,' he said, 'how can I ask for love, if I don't feel any love in myself. You know I have a real regard for you –'

'How can you feel any love, when you never feel anything?' she said.

'That is true,' he replied.

And she waited for what next.

'And how can I marry?' he said. 'I am a failure even at making money. I can't ask my mother for money.'

She sighed deeply.

'Then don't bother yet about marrying,' she said. 'Only love me a little. Won't you?'

He gave a short laugh.

'It sounds so atrocious, to say it is hard to begin,' he said.

She sighed again. He was so stiff to move.

'Shall we sit down a minute,' she said. And then as they sat on the hay, she added: 'May I touch you? Do you mind?'

'Yes, I mind! But do as you wish,' he replied, with that mixture of shyness and queer candour which made him a little ridiculous, as he knew quite well. But in his heart there was almost murder.

She touched his black, always tidy hair with her fingers.

'I suppose I shall rebel one day,' he said again, suddenly.

62

They sat some time, till it grew chilly. And he held her hand fast, but he never put his arms round her. At last she rose and went indoors, saying good night.

The next day, as Cecilia lay stunned and angry on the roof, taking her sun-bath, and becoming hot and fierce with sunshine, suddenly she started. A terror seized her in spite of herself. It was the voice.

'*Caro, caro, tu non l'hai visto!*' it was murmuring away, in a language Cecilia did not understand. She lay and writhed her limbs in the sun, listening intently to words she could not follow. Softly, whisperingly, with infinite caressiveness and yet with that subtle, insidious arrogance under its velvet, came the voice, murmuring in Italian: '*Bravo, sì molto bravo, poverino, ma uomo come te non lo sarà mai, mai, mai!*' Oh, especially in Italian Cecilia heard the poisonous charm of the voice, so caressive, so soft and flexible, yet so utterly egoistic. She hated it with intensity as it sighed and whispered out of nowhere. Why, why should it be so delicate, so subtle and flexible and beautifully controlled, while she herself was so clumsy! Oh, poor Cecilia, she writhed in the afternoon sun, knowing her own clownish clumsiness and lack of suavity, in comparison.

'No, Robert dear, you will never be the man your father was, though you have some of his looks. He was a marvellous lover, soft as a flower, yet piercing as a humming-bird. No, Robert dear, you will never know how to serve a woman as Monsignor Mauro did. *Cara, cara mia bellissima, ti ho aspettato come l'agonizzante aspetta la morte, morte deliziosa, quasi quasi troppo deliziosa per un'anima umana* – Soft as a flower, yet probing like a humming-bird. He gave himself to a woman as he gave himself to God. Mauro! Mauro! How you loved me!'

The voice ceased in reverie, and Cecilia knew what she had guessed before, that Robert was not the son of her Uncle Ronald, but of some Italian.

'I am disappointed in you, Robert. There is no poignancy in you. Your father was a Jesuit, but he was the most perfect and poignant lover in the world. You are a Jesuit like a fish

in a tank. And that Ciss of yours is the cat fishing for you.
It is less edifying even than poor Henry.'

Cecilia suddenly bent her mouth down to the tube, and
said in a deep voice:

'Leave Robert alone! Don't kill him as well.'

There was a dead silence, in the hot July afternoon that
was lowering for thunder. Cecilia lay prostrate, her heart
beating in great thumps. She was listening as if her whole
soul were an ear. At last she caught the whisper:

'Did someone speak?'

She leaned again to the mouth of the tube.

'Don't kill Robert as you killed me,' she said with slow
enunciation, and a deep but small voice.

'Ah!' came the sharp little cry. 'Who is that speaking?'

'Henry!' said the deep voice.

There was a dead silence. Poor Cecilia lay with all the use
gone out of her. And there was dead silence. Till at last
came the whisper:

'I didn't kill Henry. No, NO! Henry, surely you can't
blame me! I loved you, dearest. I only wanted to help you.'

'You killed me!' came the deep, artificial, accusing voice.
'Now, let Robert live. Let him go! Let him marry!'

There was a pause.

'How very, very awful!' mused the whispering voice. 'Is
it possible, Henry, you are a spirit, and you condemn me?'

'Yes! I condemn you!'

Cecilia felt all her pent-up rage going down that rain-pipe.
At the same time, she almost laughed. It was awful.

She lay and listened and listened. No sound! As if time
had ceased, she lay inert in the weakening sun. The sky was
yellowing. Quickly she dressed herself, went down, and out
to the corner of the stables.

'Aunt Pauline!' she called discreetly. 'Did you hear
thunder?'

'Yes! I am going in. Don't wait,' came a feeble voice.

Cecilia retired, and from the loft watched, spying, as the
figure of the lovely lady, wrapped in a lovely wrap of old
blue silk, went rather totteringly to the house.

64

The sky gradually darkened, Cecilia hastened in with the rugs. Then the storm broke. Aunt Pauline did not appear to tea. She found the thunder trying. Robert also did not arrive till after tea, in the pouring rain. Cecilia went down the covered passage to her own house, and dressed carefully for dinner, putting some white columbines at her breast.

The drawing-room was lit with a softly-shaded lamp. Robert, dressed, was waiting, listening to the rain. He too seemed strangely cracking and on edge. Cecilia came in with the white flowers nodding at her breast. Robert was watching her curiously, a new look on his face. Cecilia went to the bookshelves near the door, and was peering for something, listening acutely. She heard a rustle, then the door softly opening. And as it opened, Ciss suddenly switched on the strong electric light by the door.

Her aunt, in a dress of black lace over ivory colour, stood in the doorway. Her face was made up, but haggard with a look of unspeakable irritability, as if years of suppressed exasperation and dislike of her fellow-men had suddenly crumpled her into an old witch.

'Oh, aunt!' cried Cecilia.

'Why, mother, you're a little old lady!' came the astounded voice of Robert: like an astonished boy: as if it were a joke.

'Have you only just found it out?' snapped the old woman venomously.

'Yes! Why, I thought –' his voice tailed out in misgiving.

The haggard, old Pauline, in a frenzy of exasperation, said: 'Aren't we going down?'

She had never even noticed the excess of light, a thing she shunned. And she went downstairs almost tottering.

At table she sat with her face like a crumpled mask of unspeakable irritability. She looked old, very old, and like a witch. Robert and Cecilia fetched furtive glances at her. And Ciss, watching Robert, saw that he was so astonished and repelled by his mother's looks, that he was another man.

'What kind of a drive home did you have?' snapped Pauline, with an almost gibbering irritability.

'It rained, of course,' he said.

'How clever of you to have found that out!' said his mother, with the grisly grin of malice that had succeeded her arch smirk.

'I don't understand,' he said with quiet suavity.

'It's apparent,' said his mother, rapidly and sloppily eating her food.

She rushed through the meal like a crazy dog, to the utter consternation of the servant. And the moment it was over, she darted in a queer, crab-like way upstairs. Robert and Cecilia followed her, thunderstruck, like two conspirators.

'You pour the coffee. I loathe it! I'm going! Good night!' said the old woman, in a succession of sharp shots. And she scrambled out of the room.

There was a dead silence. At last he said:

'I'm afraid mother isn't well. I must persuade her to see a doctor.'

'Yes!' said Cecilia.

The evening passed in silence. Robert and Ciss stayed on in the drawing-room, having lit a fire. Outside was cold rain. Each pretended to read. They did not want to separate. The evening passed with ominous mysteriousness, yet quickly.

At about ten o'clock, the door suddenly opened, and Pauline appeared in a blue wrap. She shut the door behind her, and came to the fire. Then she looked at the two young people in hate, real hate.

'You two had better get married quickly,' she said in an ugly voice. 'It would look more decent; such a passionate pair of lovers!'

Robert looked up at her quietly.

'I thought you believed that cousins should not marry, mother,' he said.

'I do! But you're not cousins. Your father was an Italian priest.' Pauline held her daintily-slippered foot to the fire, in an old coquettish gesture. Her body tried to repeat all the old graceful gestures. But the nerve had snapped, so it was a rather dreadful caricature.

'Is that really true, mother?' he asked.

'True! What do you think? He was a distinguished man, or he wouldn't have been my lover. He was far too distinguished a man to have had you for a son. But that joy fell to me.'

'How unfortunate all round,' he said slowly.

'Unfortunate for you? *You* were lucky. It was *my* misfortune,' she said acidly to him.

She was really a dreadful sight, like a piece of lovely Venetian glass that has been dropped, and gathered up again in horrible, sharp-edged fragments.

Suddenly she left the room again.

For a week it went on. She did not recover. It was as if every nerve in her body had suddenly started screaming in an insanity of discordance. The doctor came, and gave her sedatives, for she never slept. Without drugs, she never slept at all, only paced back and forth in her room, looking hideous and evil, reeking with malevolence. She could not bear to see either her son or her niece. Only when either of them came, she asked in pure malice:

'Well! When's the wedding! Have you celebrated the nuptials yet?'

At first Cecilia was stunned by what she had done. She realized vaguely that her aunt, once a definite thrust of condemnation had penetrated her beautiful armour, had just collapsed squirming inside her shell. It was too terrible. Ciss was almost terrified into repentance. Then she thought: This is what she always was. Now let her live the rest of her days in her true colours.

But Pauline would not live long. She was literally shrivelling away. She kept to her room, and saw no one. She had her mirrors taken away.

Robert and Cecilia sat a good deal together. The jeering of the mad Pauline had not driven them apart, as she had hoped. But Cecilia dared not confess to him what she had done.

'Do you think your mother ever loved anybody?' Ciss asked him tentatively, rather wistfully, one evening.

He looked at her fixedly.

'Herself!' he said at last.

'She didn't even *love* herself,' said Ciss. 'It was something else – what was it?' She lifted a troubled, utterly puzzled face to him.

'Power!' he said curtly.

'But what power?' she asked. 'I don't understand.'

'Power to feed on other lives,' he said bitterly. 'She was beautiful, and she fed on life. She has fed on me as she fed on Henry. She put a sucker into one's soul and sucked up one's essential life.'

'And don't you forgive her?'

'No.'

'Poor Aunt Pauline!'

But even Ciss did not mean it. She was only aghast.

'I *know* I've got a heart,' he said, passionately striking his breast. 'But it's almost sucked dry. I *know* people who want power over others.'

Ciss was silent; what was there to say?

And two days later, Pauline was found dead in her bed, having taken too much veronal, for her heart was weakened. From the grave even she hit back at her son and her niece. She left Robert the noble sum of one thousand pounds; and Ciss one hundred. All the rest, with the nucleus of her valuable antiques, went to form the 'Pauline Attenborough Museum'.

Rawdon's Roof

RAWDON was the sort of man who said, privately, to his men friends, over a glass of wine after dinner: 'No woman shall sleep again under my roof!'

He said it with pride, rather vaunting, pursing his lips. 'Even my housekeeper goes home to sleep.'

But the housekeeper was a gentle old thing of about sixty, so it seemed a little fantastic. Moreover, the man had a wife, of whom he was secretly rather proud, as a piece of fine property, and with whom he kept up a very witty correspondence, epistolary, and whom he treated with humorous gallantry when they occasionally met for half an hour. Also he had a love affair going on. At least, if it wasn't a love affair, what was it? However!

'No, I've come to the determination that no woman shall ever sleep under my roof again – not even a female cat!'

One looked at the roof, and wondered what it had done amiss. Besides, it wasn't his roof. He only rented the house. What does a man mean, anyhow, when he says 'my roof'? *My* roof! The only roof I am conscious of having, myself, is the top of my head. However, he hardly can have meant that no woman should sleep under the elegant dome of his skull. Though there's no telling. You see the top of a sleek head through a window, and you say: 'By Jove, what a pretty girl's head!' And after all, when the individual comes out, it's in trousers.

The point, however, is that Rawdon said so emphatically – no, not emphatically, succinctly: 'No woman shall ever again sleep under my roof.' It was a case of futurity. No doubt he had had his ceilings whitewashed, and their memories put out. Or rather, repainted, for it was a handsome wooden ceiling. Anyhow, if ceilings have eyes, as walls have ears, then Rawdon had given his ceilings a new outlook, with a new coat of paint, and all memory of any woman's having slept under them – for after all, in decent circumstances we

sleep under ceilings, not under roofs – was wiped out for
ever.

'And will you neither sleep under any woman's roof?'

That pulled him up rather short. He was not prepared to
sauce his gander as he had sauced his goose. Even I could
see the thought flitting through his mind, that some of his
pleasantest holidays depended on the charm of his hostess.
Even some of the nicest hotels were run by women.

'Ah! Well! That's not quite the same thing, you know.
When one leaves one's own house one gives up the keys of
circumstance, so to speak. But, as far as possible, I make it
a rule not to sleep under a roof that is openly, and obviously,
and obtrusively a woman's roof!'

'Quite!' said I with a shudder. 'So do I!'

Now I understood his mysterious love affair less than ever.
He was never known to speak of this love affair: he did not
even write about it to his wife. The lady – for she was a lady
– lived only five minutes' walk from Rawdon. She had a
husband, but he was in diplomatic service or something like
that, which kept him occupied in the sufficiently-far distance.
Yes, far enough. And, as a husband, he was a complete
diplomat. A balance of power. If he was entitled to occupy
the wide field of the world, she, the other and contrasting
power, might concentrate and consolidate her position at
home.

She was a charming woman, too, and even a beautiful
woman. She had two charming children, long-legged, stalky,
clove-pink-half-opened sort of children. But really charming.
And she was a woman with a certain mystery. She never
talked. She never said anything about herself. Perhaps she
suffered; perhaps she was frightfully happy, and made *that*
her cause for silence. Perhaps she was wise enough even to
be beautifully silent about her happiness. Certainly she
never mentioned her sufferings, or even her trials: and
certainly she must have a fair handful of the latter, for Alec
Drummond sometimes fled home in the teeth of a gale of
debts. He simply got through his own money and through
hers, and, third and fatal stride, through other people's as

well. Then something had to be done about it. And Janet, dear soul, had to put her hat on and take journeys. But she never said anything of it. At least, she did just hint that Alec didn't *quite* make enough money to meet expenses. But after all, we don't go about with our eyes shut, and Alec Drummond, whatever else he did, didn't hide his prowess under a bushel.

Rawdon and he were quite friendly, but really! None of them ever talked. Drummond didn't talk, he just went off and behaved in his own way. And though Rawdon would chat away till the small hours, *he* never 'talked'. Not to his nearest male friend did he ever mention Janet save as a very pleasant woman and his neighbour: he admitted he adored her children. They often came to see him.

And one felt about Rawdon, he was making a mystery of something. And that was rather irritating. He went every day to see Janet, and of course we saw him going: going or coming. How can one help but see? But he always went in the morning, at about eleven, and did not stay for lunch: or he went in the afternoon, and came home to dinner. Apparently he was never there in the evening. Poor Janet, she lived like a widow.

Very well, if Rawdon wanted to make it so blatantly obvious that it was only platonic, purely platonic, why wasn't he natural? Why didn't he say simply: 'I'm very fond of Janet Drummond, she is my very dear friend?' Why did he sort of curl up at the very mention of her name, and curdle into silence: or else say rather forcedly: 'Yes, she is a charming woman. I see a good deal of her, but chiefly for the children's sake. I'm devoted to the children!' Then he would look at one in such a curious way, as if he were hiding something. And after all, what was there to hide? If he was the woman's friend, why not? It could be a charming friendship. And if he were her lover, why, heaven bless me, he ought to have been proud of it, and showed just a glint, just an honest man's glint.

But no, never a glint of pride or pleasure in the relation either way. Instead of that, this rather theatrical reserve. Janet, it is true, was just as reserved. If she could, she avoided mentioning his name. Yet one knew, sure as houses, she felt something. One suspected her of being more in love with Rawdon than ever she had been with Alec. And one felt that there was a hush upon it all. She had had a hush put upon her. By whom? By both the men? Or by Rawdon only? Or by Drummond? Was it for her husband's sake? Impossible! For the children's? But why! Her children were devoted to Rawdon.

It now had become the custom for them to go to him three times a week, for music. I don't mean he taught them the piano. Rawdon was a very refined musical amateur. He had them sing, in their delicate girlish voices, delicate little songs, and really he succeeded wonderfully with them; he made them so true, which children rarely are, musically, and so pure and effortless, like little flamelets of sound. It really was rather beautiful, and sweet of him. And he taught them *music*, the delicacy of the feel of it. They had a regular teacher for the practice.

Even the little girls, in their young little ways, were in love with Rawdon! So if their mother were in love too, in her ripened womanhood, why not?

Poor Janet! She was so still, and so elusive: the hush upon her! She was rather like a half-opened rose that somebody had tied a string round, so that it couldn't open any more. But why? Why? In her there was a real touch of mystery. One could never *ask* her, because one knew her heart was too keenly involved: or her pride.

Whereas there was, really, no mystery about Rawdon, refined and handsome and subtle as he was. He *had* no mystery: at least, to a man. What *he* wrapped himself up in was a certain amount of mystification.

Who wouldn't be irritated to hear a fellow saying, when for months and months he has been paying a daily visit to a lonely and very attractive woman – nay, lately even a twice-daily visit, even if always before sundown – to hear him say, pursing his lips after a sip of his own very moderate port: 'I've taken a vow that no women shall sleep under my roof again!'

I almost snapped out: 'Oh, what the hell! And what about your Janet?' But I remembered in time, it was not *my* affair,

72

and if he wanted to have his mystifications, let him have them.

If he meant he wouldn't have his wife sleep under his roof again, that one could understand. They were really very witty with one another, he and she, but fatally and damnably married.

Yet neither wanted a divorce. And neither put the slightest claim to any control over the other's behaviour. He said: 'Women live on the moon, men on the earth.' And she said: 'I don't mind in the least if he loves Janet Drummond, poor thing. It would be a change for him, from loving himself. And a change for her, if somebody loved her –'

Poor Janet! But he wouldn't have her sleep under his roof, no, not for any money. And apparently he never slept under hers – if she could be said to have one. So what the deuce?

Of course, if they were friends, just friends, all right! But then in that case, why start talking about not having a woman sleep under your roof? Pure mystification!

The cat never came out of the bag. But one evening I distinctly heard it mewing inside its sack, and I even believe I saw a claw through the canvas.

It was in November – everything much as usual – myself pricking my ears to hear if the rain had stopped, and I could go home, because I was just a little bored about 'cornemuse' music. I had been having dinner with Rawdon, and listening to him ever since on his favourite topic: not, of course, women, and why they shouldn't sleep under his roof, but fourteenth-century melody and windbag accompaniment.

It was not late – not yet ten o'clock – but I was restless, and wanted to go home. There was no longer any sound of rain. And Rawdon was perhaps going to make a pause in his monologue.

Suddenly there was a tap at the door, and Rawdon's man, Hawken, edged in. Rawdon, who had been a major in some fantastic capacity during the war, had brought Hawken back with him. This fresh-faced man of about thirty-five appeared in the doorway with an intensely blank and bewildered look on his face. He was really an extraordinarily good actor.

'A lady, sir!' he said, with a look of utter blankness.

'A what?' snapped Rawdon.

'A lady!' – then with a most discreet drop in his voice: 'Mrs Drummond, sir!' He looked modestly down at his feet.

Rawdon went deathly white, and his lips quivered.

'Mrs Drummond! Where?'

Hawken lifted his eyes to his master in a fleeting glance.

'I showed her into the dining-room, there being no fire in the drawing-room.'

Rawdon got to his feet and took two or three agitated strides. He could not make up his mind. At last he said, his lips working with agitation:

'Bring her in here.'

Then he turned with a theatrical gesture to me.

'What this is all about, I *don't* know,' he said.

'Let me clear out,' said I, making for the door.

He caught me by the arm.

'No, for God's sake! For God's sake, stop and see me through!'

He gripped my arm till it really hurt, and his eyes were quite wild. I did not know my Olympic Rawdon.

Hastily I backed away to the side of the fire – we were in Rawdon's room, where the books and piano were – and Mrs Drummond appeared in the doorway. She was much paler than usual, being a rather warm-coloured woman, and she glanced at me with big reproachful eyes, as much as to say: You intruder! You interloper! For my part, I could do nothing but stare. She wore a black wrap, which I knew quite well, over her black dinner-dress.

'Rawdon!' she said, turning to him and blotting out my existence from her consciousness. Hawken softly closed the door, and I could *feel* him standing on the threshold outside, listening keen as a hawk.

'Sit down, Janet,' said Rawdon, with a grimace of a sour smile, which he could not get rid of once he had started it, so that his face looked very odd indeed, like a mask which he was unable either to fit on or take off. He had several conflicting expressions all at once, and they had all stuck.

She let her wrap slip back on her shoulders, and knitted her white fingers against her skirt, pressing down her arms, and gazing at him with a terrible gaze. I began to creep to the door.

Rawdon started after me.

'No, don't go! Don't go! I specially want you not to go,' he said in extreme agitation.

I looked at her. She was looking at him with a heavy, sombre kind of stare. Me she absolutely ignored. Not for a second could she forgive me for existing on the earth. I slunk back to my post behind the leather arm-chair, as if hiding.

'Do sit down, Janet,' he said to her again. 'And have a smoke. What will you drink?'

'No, thanks!' she said, as if it were one word slurred out. 'No, thanks.'

And she proceeded again to fix him with that heavy, portentous stare.

He offered her a cigarette, his hand trembling as he held out the silver box.

'No thanks!' she slurred out again, not even looking at the box, but keeping him fixed with that dark and heavy stare.

He turned away, making a great delay lighting a cigarette, with his back to her, to get out of the stream of that stare. He carefully went for an ash-tray, and put it carefully within reach – all the time trying not to be swept away on that stare. And she stood with her fingers locked, her straight, plump, handsome arms pressed downwards against her skirt, and she gazed at him.

He leaned his elbow on the mantelpiece abstractedly for a moment – then he started suddenly, and rang the bell. She turned her eyes from him for a moment, to watch his middle finger pressing the bell-button. Then there was a tension of waiting, an interruption in the previous tension. We waited. Nobody came. Rawdon rang again.

'That's very curious!' he murmured to himself. Hawken was usually so prompt. Hawken, not being a woman, slept under the roof, so there was no excuse for his not answering the bell. The tension in the room had now changed quality, owing to this new suspense. Poor Janet's sombre stare became gradually loosened, so to speak. Attention was divided. Where was Hawken? Rawdon rang the bell a third time, a long peal. And now Janet was no longer the centre of suspense. Where was Hawken? The question loomed large over every other.

'I'll just look in the kitchen,' said I, making for the door.

'No, no. I'll go,' said Rawdon.

But I was in the passage – and Rawdon was on my heels.

The kitchen was very tidy and cheerful, but empty; only a bottle of beer and two glasses stood on the table. To Rawdon the kitchen was as strange a world as to me – he never entered the servants' quarters. But to me it was curious that the bottle of beer was empty, and both the glasses had been used. I knew Rawdon wouldn't notice.

'That's very curious!' said Rawdon: meaning the absence of his man.

At that moment we heard a step on the servants' stairs, and Rawdon opened the door, to reveal Hawken descending with an armful of sheets and things.

'What are you doing?'

'Why! –' and a pause. 'I was airing the clean laundry, like – not to waste the fire last thing.'

Hawken descended into the kitchen with a very flushed face and very bright eyes and rather ruffled hair, and proceeded to spread the linen on chairs before the fire.

'I hope I've not done wrong, sir,' he said in his most winning manner. 'Was you ringing?'

'Three times! Leave that linen and bring a bottle of the fizz.'

'I'm sorry, sir. You can't hear the bell from the front, sir.'

It was perfectly true. The house was small, but it had been built for a very nervous author, and the servants' quarters were shut off, padded off from the rest of the house.

Rawdon said no more about the sheets and things, but he looked more peaked than ever.

We went back to the music-room. Janet had gone to the hearth, and stood with her hand on the mantel. She looked round at us, baffled.

'We're having a bottle of fizz,' said Rawdon. 'Do let me take your wrap.'

'And where was Hawken?' she asked satirically.

'Oh, busy somewhere upstairs.'

'He's a busy young man, that!' she said sardonically. And she sat uncomfortably on the edge of the chair where I had been sitting.

When Hawken came with the tray, she said:

'I'm not going to drink.'

Rawdon appealed to me, so I took a glass. She looked inquiringly at the flushed and bright-eyed Hawken, as if she understood something.

The manservant left the room. We drank our wine, and the awkwardness returned.

'Rawdon!' she said suddenly, as if she were firing a revolver at him. 'Alec came home tonight in a bigger mess than ever, and wanted to make love to me to get it off his mind. I can't stand it any more. I'm in love with you, and I simply can't stand Alec getting too near to me. He's dangerous when he's crossed – and when he's worked up. So I just came here. I didn't see what else I could do.'

She left off as suddenly as a machine-gun leaves off firing. We were just dazed.

'You are quite right,' Rawdon began, in a vague and neutral tone . . .

'I am, am I not?' she said eagerly.

'I'll tell you what I'll do,' he said. 'I'll go round to the hotel tonight, and you can stay here.'

'Under the kindly protection of Hawken, you mean!' she said, with quiet sarcasm.

'Why! – I could send Mrs Betts, I suppose,' he said.

Mrs Betts was his housekeeper.

'You couldn't stay and protect me yourself?' she said quietly.

'I! I! Why, I've made a vow – haven't I, Joe?' – he turned to me – 'not to have any women sleep under my roof again.' – He got the mixed sour smile on his face.

She looked up at the ceiling for a moment, then lapsed into silence. Then she said:

'Sort of monastery, so to speak!'

And she rose and reached for her wrap, adding:

'I'd better go, then.'

'Joe will see you home,' he said.

She faced round on me.

'Do you mind *not* seeing me home, Mr Bradley?' she said, gazing at me.

'Not if you don't want me,' said I.

'Hawken will drive you,' said Rawdon.

'Oh, no, he won't!' she said. 'I'll walk. Good night.'

'I'll get my hat,' stammered Rawdon, in an agony. 'Wait! Wait! The gate will be locked.'

'It was open when I came,' she said.

He rang for Hawken to unlock the iron doors at the end of the short drive, whilst he himself huddled into a greatcoat and scarf, fumbling for a flashlight.

'You won't go till I come back, will you?' he pleaded to me. 'I'd be awfully glad if you'd stay the night. The sheets *will* be aired.'

I had to promise – and he set off with an umbrella, in the rain, at the same time asking Hawken to take a flashlight and go in front. So that was how they went, in single file along the path over the fields to Mrs Drummond's house, Hawken in front, with flashlight and umbrella, curving round to light up in front of Mrs Drummond, who, with umbrella only, walked isolated between two lights, Rawdon shining his flashlight on her from the rear from under his umbrella. I turned indoors.

So that was over! At least, for the moment!

I thought I would go upstairs and see how damp the bed in the guest-chamber was before I actually stayed the night with Rawdon. He never had guests – preferred to go away himself.

The guest-chamber was a good room across a passage and round a corner from Rawdon's room – its door just opposite the padded service-door. This latter service-door stood open, and a light shone through. I went into the spare bedroom, switching on the light.

To my surprise, the bed looked as if it had just been left – the sheets tumbled, the pillows pressed. I put in my hands under the bedclothes, and it was warm. Very curious!

As I stood looking round in mild wonder, I heard a voice call softly: 'Joe!'

'Yes!' said I instinctively, and, though startled, strode at once out of the room and through the servants' door, towards the voice. Light shone from the open doorway of one of the servants' rooms.

There was a muffled little shriek, and I was standing looking into what was probably Hawken's bedroom, and seeing a soft and pretty white leg and a very pretty feminine posterior very thinly dimmed in a rather short night-dress, just in the act of climbing into a narrow little bed, and, then arrested, the owner of the pretty posterior burying her face in the bedclothes, to be invisible, like the ostrich in the sand.

I discreetly withdrew, went downstairs and poured myself a glass of wine. And very shortly Rawdon returned looking like Hamlet in the last act.

He said nothing, neither did I. We sat and merely smoked. Only as he was seeing me upstairs to bed, in the now immaculate bedroom, he said pathetically:

'Why aren't women content to be what a man wants them to be?'

'Why aren't they!' said I wearily.

'I thought I had made everything clear,' he said.

'You start at the wrong end,' said I.

And as I said it, the picture came into my mind of the pretty feminine butt-end in Hawken's bedroom. Yes, Hawken made better starts, wherever he ended.

When he brought me my cup of tea in the morning, he was very soft and cat-like. I asked him what sort of day it was, and he asked me if I'd had a good night, and was I comfortable.

'Very comfortable!' said I. 'But I turned you out, I'm afraid.'

'Me, sir?' He turned on me a face of utter bewilderment. But I looked him in the eye.

'Is your name Joe?' I asked him.

'You're right, sir.'

'So is mine,' said I. 'However, I didn't see her face, so it's all right. I suppose you *were* a bit tight, in that little bed!'

'Well, sir!' and he flashed me a smile of amazing impudence, and lowered his tone to utter confidence. 'This is the best bed in the house, this is.' And he touched it softly.

'You've not tried them all, surely?'

A look of indignant horror on his face!

'No, sir, indeed I haven't.'

That day, Rawdon left for London, on his way to Tunis, and Hawken was to follow him. The roof of his house looked just the same.

The Drummonds moved too – went away somewhere, and left a lot of unsatisfied tradespeople behind.

The Rocking-Horse Winner

THERE was a woman who was beautiful, who started with all the advantages, yet she had no luck. She married for love, and the love turned to dust. She had bonny children, yet she felt they had been thrust upon her, and she could not love them. They looked at her coldly, as if they were finding fault with her. And hurriedly she felt she must cover up some fault in herself. Yet what it was that she must cover up she never knew. Nevertheless, when her children were present, she always felt the centre of her heart go hard. This troubled her, and in her manner she was all the more gentle and anxious for her children, as if she loved them very much. Only she herself knew that at the centre of her heart was a hard little place that could not feel love, no, not for anybody. Everybody else said of her: 'She is such a good mother. She adores her children.' Only she herself, and her children themselves, know it was not so. They read it in each other's eyes.

There were a boy and two little girls. They lived in a pleasant house, with a garden, and they had discreet servants, and felt themselves superior to anyone in the neighbourhood.

Although they lived in style, they felt always an anxiety in the house. There was never enough money. The mother had a small income, and the father had a small income, but not nearly enough for the social position which they had to keep up. The father went into town to some office. But though he had good prospects, these prospects never materialized. There was always the grinding sense of the shortage of money, though the style was always kept up.

At last the mother said: 'I will see if *I* can't make something.' But she did not know where to begin. She racked her brains, and tried this thing and the other, but could not find anything successful. The failure made deep lines come into her face. Her children were growing up, they would have to go to school. There must be more money, there must be more money. The father, who was always very handsome and expensive in his tastes, seemed as if he never *would* be able to do anything worth doing. And the mother, who had a great belief in herself, did not succeed any better, and her tastes were just as expensive.

And so the house came to be haunted by the unspoken phrase: *There must be more money! There must be more money!* The children could hear it all the time, though nobody said it aloud. They heard it at Christmas, when the expensive and splendid toys filled the nursery. Behind the shining modern rocking-horse, behind the smart doll's house, a voice would start whispering: 'There *must* be more money! There *must* be more money!' And the children would stop playing, to listen for a moment. They would look into each other's eyes, to see if they had all heard. And each one saw in the eyes of the other two that they too had heard. 'There *must* be more money! There *must* be more money!'

It came whispering from the springs of the still-swaying rocking-horse, and even the horse, bending his wooden, champing head, heard it. The big doll, sitting so pink and smirking in her new pram, could hear it quite plainly, and seemed to be smirking all the more self-consciously because of it. The foolish puppy, too, that took the place of the teddy-bear, he was looking so extraordinarily foolish for no other reason but that he heard the secret whisper all over the house: 'There *must* be more money!'

Yet nobody ever said it aloud. The whisper was everywhere, and therefore no one spoke it. Just as no one ever says: 'We are breathing!' in spite of the fact that breath is coming and going all the time.

'Mother,' said the boy Paul one day, 'why don't we keep a car of our own? Why do we always use uncle's, or else a taxi?'

'Because we're the poor members of the family,' said the mother.

'But why *are* we, mother?'

'Well – I suppose,' she said slowly and bitterly, 'it's because your father had no luck.'

The boy was silent for some time.

'Is luck money, mother?' he asked, rather timidly.

'No, Paul. Not quite. It's what causes you to have money.'

'Oh!' said Paul vaguely. 'I thought when Uncle Oscar said *filthy lucker,* it meant money.'

'*Filthy lucre* does mean money,' said the mother. 'But it's lucre, not luck.'

'Oh!' said the boy. 'Then what *is* luck, mother?'

'It's what causes you to have money. If you're lucky you have money. That's why it's better to be born lucky than rich. If you're rich, you may lose your money. But if you're lucky, you will always get more money.'

'Oh! Will you? And is father not lucky?'

'Very unlucky, I should say,' she said bitterly.

The boy watched her with unsure eyes.

'Why?' he asked.

'I don't know. Nobody ever knows why one person is lucky and another unlucky.'

'Don't they? Nobody at all? Does *nobody* know?'

'Perhaps God. But He never tells.'

'He ought to, then. And aren't you lucky either, mother?'

'I can't be, if I married an unlucky husband.'

'But by yourself, aren't you?'

'I used to think I was, before I married. Now I think I am very unlucky indeed.'

'Why?'

'Well – never mind! Perhaps I'm not really,' she said.

The child looked at her to see if she meant it. But he saw, by the lines of her mouth, that she was only trying to hide something from him.

'Well, anyhow,' he said stoutly, 'I'm a lucky person.'

'Why?' said his mother, with a sudden laugh.

He stared at her. He didn't even know why he had said it.

'God told me,' he asserted, brazening it out.

'I hope He did, dear!' she said, again with a laugh, but rather bitter.

'He did, mother!'

'Excellent!' said the mother, using one of her husband's exclamations.

The boy saw she did not believe him; or rather, that she

paid no attention to his assertion. This angered him some-where, and made him want to compel her attention.

He went off by himself, vaguely, in a childish way, seeking for the clue to 'luck'. Absorbed, taking no heed of other people, he went about with a sort of stealth, seeking inwardly for luck. He wanted luck, he wanted it, he wanted it. When the two girls were playing dolls in the nursery, he would sit on his big rocking-horse, charging madly into space, with a frenzy that made the little girls peer at him uneasily. Wildly the horse careered, the waving dark hair of the boy tossed, his eyes had a strange glare in them. The little girls dared not speak to him.

When he had ridden to the end of his mad little journey, he climbed down and stood in front of his rocking-horse, staring fixedly into its lowered face. Its red mouth was slightly open, its big eye was wide and glassy-bright.

'Now!' he would silently command the snorting steed. 'Now, take me to where there is luck! Now take me!'

And he would slash the horse on the neck with the little whip he had asked Uncle Oscar for. He *knew* the horse could take him to where there was luck, if only he forced it. So he would mount again and start on his furious ride, hoping at last to get there. He knew he could get there.

'You'll break your horse, Paul!' said the nurse.

'He's always riding like that! I wish he'd leave off!' said his elder sister Joan.

But he only glared down on them in silence. Nurse gave him up. She could make nothing of him. Anyhow, he was growing beyond her.

One day his mother and his Uncle Oscar came in when he was on one of his furious rides. He did not speak to them.

'Hallo, you young jockey! Riding a winner?' said his uncle.

'Aren't you growing too big for a rocking-horse? You're not a very little boy any longer, you know,' said his mother.

But Paul only gave a blue glare from his big, rather close-set eyes. He would speak to nobody when he was in full tilt. His mother watched him with an anxious expression on her face.

At last he suddenly stopped forcing his horse into the mechanical gallop and slid down.

'Well, I got there!' he announced fiercely, his blue eyes still flaring, and his sturdy long legs straddling apart.

'Where did you get to?' asked his mother.

'Where I wanted to go.' he flared back at her.

'That's right, son!' said Uncle Oscar. 'Don't you stop till you get there. What's the horse's name?'

'He doesn't have a name,' said the boy.

'Gets on without all right?' asked the uncle.

'Well, he has different names. He was called Sansovino last week.'

'Sansovino, eh? Won the Ascot. How did you know this name?'

'He always talks about horse-races with Bassett,' said Joan.

The uncle was delighted to find that his small nephew was posted with all the racing news. Bassett, the young gardener, who had been wounded in the left foot in the war and had got his present job through Oscar Cresswell, whose batman he had been, was a perfect blade of the 'turf'. He lived in the racing events, and the small boy lived with him.

Oscar Cresswell got it all from Bassett.

'Master Paul comes and asks me, so I can't do more than tell him, sir,' said Bassett, his face terribly serious, as if he were speaking of religious matters.

'And does he ever put anything on a horse he fancies?'

'Well – I don't want to give him away – he's a young sport, a fine sport, sir. Would you mind asking him himself? He sort of takes a pleasure in it, and perhaps he'd feel I was giving him away, sir, if you don't mind.'

Bassett was serious as a church.

The uncle went back to his nephew and took him off for a ride in the car.

'Say, Paul, old man, do you ever put anything on a horse?' the uncle asked.

The boy watched the handsome man closely.

'Why, do you think I oughtn't to?' he parried.

'Not a bit of it! I thought perhaps you might give me a tip for the Lincoln.'

The car sped on into the country, going down to Uncle Oscar's place in Hampshire.

'Honour bright?' said the nephew.

'Honour bright, son!' said the uncle.

'Well, then, Daffodil.'

'Daffodil! I doubt it, sonny. What about Mirza?'

'I only know the winner,' said the boy. 'That's Daffodil.'

'Daffodil, eh?'

There was a pause. Daffodil was an obscure horse comparatively.

'Uncle!'

'Yes, son?'

'You won't let it go any further, will you? I promised Bassett.'

'Bassett be damned, old man! What's he got to do with it?'

'We're partners. We've been partners from the first. Uncle, he lent me my first five shillings, which I lost. I promised him, honour bright, it was only between me and him; only you gave me that ten-shilling note I started winning with, so I thought you were lucky. You won't let it go any further, will you?'

The boy gazed at his uncle from those big, hot, blue eyes, set rather close together. The uncle stirred and laughed uneasily.

'Right you are, son! I'll keep your tip private. Daffodil, eh? How much are you putting on him?'

'All except twenty pounds,' said the boy. 'I keep that in reserve.'

The uncle thought it a good joke.

'You keep twenty pounds in reserve, do you, you young romancer? What are you betting, then?'

'I'm betting three hundred,' said the boy gravely. 'But it's between you and me, Uncle Oscar! Honour bright?'

The uncle burst into a roar of laughter.

'It's between you and me all right, you young Nat Gould,' he said, laughing. 'But where's your three hundred?'

'Bassett keeps it for me. We're partners.'

'You are, are you! And what is Bassett putting on Daffodil?'

'He won't go quite as high as I do, I expect. Perhaps he'll go a hundred and fifty.'

'What, pennies?' laughed the uncle.

'Pounds,' said the child, with a surprised look at his uncle. 'Bassett keeps a bigger reserve than I do.'

Between wonder and amusement Uncle Oscar was silent. He pursued the matter no further, but he determined to take his nephew with him to the Lincoln races.

'Now, son,' he said, 'I'm putting twenty on Mirza, and I'll put five on for you on any horse you fancy. What's your pick?'

'Daffodil, uncle.'

'No, not the fiver on Daffodil!'

'I should if it was my own fiver,' said the child.

'Good! Good! Right you are! A fiver for me and a fiver for you on Daffodil.'

The child had never been to a race-meeting before, and his eyes were blue fire. He pursed his mouth tight and watched. A Frenchman just in front had put his money on Lancelot. Wild with excitement, he flayed his arms up and down, yelling '*Lancelot! Lancelot!*' in his French accent.

Daffodil came in first, Lancelot second, Mirza third. The child, flushed and with eyes blazing, was curiously serene. His uncle brought him four five-pound notes, four to one.

'What am I to do with these?' he cried, waving them before the boy's eyes.

'I suppose we'll talk to Bassett,' said the boy. 'I expect I have fifteen hundred now; and twenty in reserve; and this twenty.'

His uncle studied him for some moments.

'Look here, son!' he said. 'You're not serious about Bassett and that fifteen hundred, are you?'

'Yes, I am. But it's between you and me, uncle. Honour bright?'

'Honour bright all right, son! But I must talk to Bassett.'

'If you'd like to be a partner, uncle, with Bassett and me, we could all be partners. Only, you'd have to promise, honour bright, uncle, not to let it go beyond us three. Bassett and I are lucky, and you must be lucky, because it was your ten shillings I started winning with ...'

Uncle Oscar took both Bassett and Paul into Richmond Park for an afternoon, and there they talked.

'It's like this, you see, sir,' Bassett said. 'Master Paul would get me talking about racing events, spinning yarns, you know, sir. And he was always keen on knowing if I'd made or if I'd lost. It's about a year since, now, that I put five shillings on Blush of Dawn for him: and we lost. Then the luck turned, with that ten shillings he had from you: that we put on Singhalese. And since that time, it's been pretty steady, all things considering. What do you say, Master Paul?'

'We're all right when we're sure,' said Paul. 'It's when we're not quite sure that we go down.'

'Oh, but we're careful then,' said Bassett.

'But when are you *sure*?' smiled Uncle Oscar.

'It's Master Paul, sir,' said Bassett in a secret, religious voice. 'It's as if he had it from heaven. Like Daffodil, now, for the Lincoln. That was as sure as eggs.'

'Did you put anything on Daffodil?' asked Oscar Cresswell.

'Yes, sir. I made my bit.'

'And my nephew?'

Bassett was obstinately silent, looking at Paul.

'I made twelve hundred, didn't I, Bassett? I told uncle I was putting three hundred on Daffodil.'

'That's right,' said Bassett, nodding.

'But where's the money?' asked the uncle.

'I keep it safe locked up, sir. Master Paul he can have it any minute he likes to ask for it.'

'What, fifteen hundred pounds?'

'And twenty! And *forty*, that is, with the twenty he made on the course.'

'It's amazing!' said the uncle.

'If Master Paul offers you to be partners, sir, I would, if I were you: if you'll excuse me,' said Bassett.

Oscar Cresswell thought about it.

'I'll see the money,' he said.

They drove home again, and, sure enough, Bassett came round to the garden-house with fifteen hundred pounds in notes. The twenty pounds reserve was left with Joe Glee, in the Turf Commission deposit.

'You see, it's all right, uncle, when I'm *sure*! Then we go strong, for all we're worth. Don't we, Bassett?'

'We do that, Master Paul.'

'And when are you sure?' said the uncle, laughing.

'Oh, well, sometimes I'm *absolutely* sure, like about Daffodil,' said the boy; 'and sometimes I have an idea; and sometimes I haven't even an idea, have I, Bassett? Then we're careful, because we mostly go down.'

'You do, do you! And when you're sure, like about Daffodil, what makes you sure, sonny?'

'Oh, well, I don't know,' said the boy uneasily. 'I'm sure, you know, uncle; that's all.'

'It's as if he had it from heaven, sir,' Bassett reiterated.

'I should say so!' said the uncle.

But he became a partner. And when the Leger was coming on Paul was 'sure' about Lively Spark, which was a quite inconsiderable horse. The boy insisted on putting a thousand on the horse, Bassett went for five hundred, and Oscar Cresswell two hundred. Lively Spark came in first, and the betting had been ten to one against him. Paul had made ten thousand.

'You see,' he said, 'I was absolutely sure of him.'

Even Oscar Cresswell had cleared two thousand.

'Look here, son,' he said, 'this sort of thing makes me nervous.'

'It needn't, uncle! Perhaps I shan't be sure again for a long time.'

'But what are you going to do with your money?' asked the uncle.

'Of course,' said the boy, 'I started it for mother. She said she had no luck, because father is unlucky, so I thought if *I* was lucky, it might stop whispering.'

'What might stop whispering?'

'Our house. I *hate* our house for whispering.'

89

'What does it whisper?'

'Why – why' – the boy fidgeted – 'why, I don't know. But it's always short of money, you know, uncle.'

'I know it, son, I know it.'

'You know people send mother writs, don't you, uncle?'

'I'm afraid I do,' said the uncle.

'And then the house whispers, like people laughing at you behind your back. It's awful, that is! I thought if I was lucky –'

'You might stop it,' added the uncle.

The boy watched him with big blue eyes, that had an uncanny cold fire in them, and he said never a word.

'Well, then!' said the uncle. 'What are we doing?'

'I shouldn't like mother to know I was lucky,' said the boy.

'Why not, son?'

'She'd stop me.'

'I don't think she would.'

'Oh!' – and the boy writhed in an odd way – 'I *don't* want her to know, uncle.'

'All right, son! We'll manage it without her knowing.'

They managed it very easily. Paul, at the other's suggestion, handed over five thousand pounds to his uncle, who deposited it with the family lawyer, who was then to inform Paul's mother that a relative had put five thousand pounds into his hands, which sum was to be paid out a thousand pounds at a time, on the mother's birthday, for the next five years.

'So she'll have a birthday present of a thousand pounds for five successive years,' said Uncle Oscar. 'I hope it won't make it all the harder for her later.'

Paul's mother had her birthday in November. The house had been 'whispering' worse than ever lately, and, even in spite of his luck, Paul could not bear up against it. He was very anxious to see the effect of the birthday letter, telling his mother about the thousand pounds.

When there were no visitors, Paul now took his meals with his parents, as he was beyond the nursery control. His mother went into town nearly every day. She had discovered that she had an odd knack of sketching furs and dress materials, so she worked secretly in the studio of a friend who was the chief 'artist' for the leading drapers. She drew the figures of ladies in furs and ladies in silk and sequins for the newspaper advertisements. This young woman artist earned several thousand pounds a year, but Paul's mother only made several hundreds, and she was again dissatisfied. She so wanted to be first in something, and she did not succeed, even in making sketches for drapery advertisements.

She was down to breakfast on the morning of her birthday. Paul watched her face as she read her letters. He knew the lawyer's letter. As his mother read it, her face hardened and became more expressionless. Then a cold, determined look came on her mouth. She hid the letter under the pile of others, and said not a word about it.

'Didn't you have anything nice in the post for your birthday, mother?' said Paul.

'Quite moderately nice,' she said, her voice cold and absent.

She went away to town without saying more.

But in the afternoon Uncle Oscar appeared. He said Paul's mother had had a long interview with the lawyer, asking if the whole five thousand could not be advanced at once, as she was in debt.

'What do you think, uncle?' said the boy.

'I leave it to you, son.'

'Oh, let her have it, then! We can get some more with the other,' said the boy.

'A bird in the hand is worth two in the bush, laddie!' said Uncle Oscar.

'But I'm sure to *know* for the Grand National; or the Lincolnshire; or else the Derby. I'm sure to know for *one* of them,' said Paul.

So Uncle Oscar signed the agreement, and Paul's mother touched the whole five thousand. Then something very curious happened. The voices in the house suddenly went mad, like a chorus of frogs on a spring evening. There were certain new furnishings, and Paul had a tutor. He was *really* going to Eton, his father's school, in the following autumn. There were flowers in the winter, and a blossoming of the luxury Paul's mother had been used to. And yet the voices in the house,

LOVE AMONG THE HAYSTACKS

behind the sprays of mimosa and almond-blossom, and from under the piles of iridescent cushions, simply trilled and screamed in a sort of ecstasy: 'There *must* be more money! Oh-h-h; there *must* be more money. Oh, now, now-w! Now-w-w – there *must* be more money! – more than ever! More than ever!'

It frightened Paul terribly. He studied away at his Latin and Greek with his tutor. But his intense hours were spent with Bassett. The Grand National had gone by; he had not 'known', and had lost a hundred pounds. Summer was at hand. He was in agony for the Lincoln. But even for the Lincoln he didn't 'know', and he lost fifty pounds. He became wild-eyed and strange, as if something were going to explode in him.

'Let it alone, son! Don't you bother about it!' urged Uncle Oscar. But it was as if the boy couldn't really hear what his uncle was saying.

'I've got to know for the Derby! I've got to know for the Derby!' the child reiterated, his big blue eyes blazing with a sort of madness.

His mother noticed how overwrought he was.

'You'd better go to the seaside. Wouldn't you like to go now to the seaside, instead of waiting? I think you'd better,' she said, looking down at him anxiously, her heart curiously heavy because of him.

But the child lifted his uncanny blue eyes.

'I couldn't possibly go before the Derby, mother!' he said. 'I couldn't possibly!'

'Why not?' she said, her voice becoming heavy when she was opposed. 'Why not? You can still go from the seaside to see the Derby with your Uncle Oscar, if that's what you wish. No need for you to wait here. Besides, I think you care too much about these races. It's a bad sign. My family has been a gambling family, and you won't know till you grow up how much damage it has done. But it has done damage. I shall have to send Bassett away, and ask Uncle Oscar not to talk racing to you, unless you promise to be reasonable about it: go away to the seaside and forget it. You're all nerves!'

'I'll do what you like, mother, so long as you don't send me away till after the Derby,' the boy said.

'Send you away from where? Just from this house?'

'Yes,' he said, gazing at her.

'Why, you curious child, what makes you care about this house so much, suddenly? I never knew you loved it.'

He gazed at her without speaking. He had a secret within a secret, something he had not divulged, even to Bassett or to his Uncle Oscar.

But his mother, after standing undecided and a little bit sullen for some moments, said:

'Very well, then! Don't go to the seaside till after the Derby, if you don't wish it. But promise me you won't let your nerves go to pieces. Promise you won't think so much about horse-racing, and *events*, as you call them!'

'Oh no,' said the boy casually. 'I won't think much about them, mother. You needn't worry. I wouldn't worry, mother, if I were you.'

'If you were me and I were you,' said his mother, 'I wonder what we *should* do!'

'But you know you needn't worry, mother, don't you?' the boy repeated.

'I should be awfully glad to know it,' she said wearily.

'Oh, well, you *can*, you know. I mean, you *ought* to know you needn't worry,' he insisted.

'Ought I? Then I'll see about it,' she said.

Paul's secret of secrets was his wooden horse, that which had no name. Since he was emancipated from a nurse and a nursery-governess, he had had his rocking-horse removed to his own bedroom at the top of the house.

'Surely you're too big for a rocking-horse!' his mother had remonstrated.

'Well, you see, mother, till I can have a *real* horse, I like to have *some* sort of animal about,' had been his quaint answer.

'Do you feel he keeps you company?' she laughed.

'Oh yes! He's very good, he always keeps me company, when I'm there,' said Paul.

So the horse, rather shabby, stood in an arrested prance in the boy's bedroom.

The Derby was drawing near, and the boy grew more and more tense. He hardly heard what was spoken to him, he was very frail, and his eyes were really uncanny. His mother had sudden strange seizures of uneasiness about him. Sometimes, for half an hour, she would feel a sudden anxiety about him that was almost anguish. She wanted to rush to him at once, and know he was safe.

Two nights before the Derby, she was at a big party in town, when one of her rushes of anxiety about her boy, her first-born, gripped her heart till she could hardly speak. She fought with the feeling, might and main, for she believed in common sense. But it was too strong. She had to leave the dance and go downstairs to telephone to the country. The children's nursery-governess was terribly surprised and startled at being rung up in the night.

'Are the children all right, Miss Wilmot?'

'Oh yes, they are quite all right.'

'Master Paul? Is he all right?'

'He went to bed as right as a trivet. Shall I run up and look at him?'

'No,' said Paul's mother reluctantly. 'No! Don't trouble. It's all right. Don't sit up. We shall be home fairly soon.' She did not want her son's privacy intruded upon.

'Very good,' said the governess.

It was about one o'clock when Paul's mother and father drove up to their house. All was still. Paul's mother went to her room and slipped off her white fur cloak. She had told her maid not to wait up for her. She heard her husband downstairs, mixing a whisky and soda.

And then, because of the strange anxiety at her heart, she stole upstairs to her son's room. Noiselessly she went along the upper corridor. Was there a faint noise? What was it?

She stood, with arrested muscles, outside his door, listening. There was a strange, heavy, and yet not loud noise. Her heart stood still. It was a soundless noise, yet rushing and powerful. Something huge, in violent, hushed motion. What was it?

What in God's name was it? She ought to know. She felt that she knew the noise. She knew what it was.

Yet she could not place it. She couldn't say what it was. And on and on it went, like a madness.

Softly, frozen with anxiety and fear, she turned the door-handle.

The room was dark. Yet in the space near the window, she heard and saw something plunging to and fro. She gazed in fear and amazement.

Then suddenly she switched on the light, and saw her son, in his green pyjamas, madly surging on the rocking-horse. The blaze of light suddenly lit him up, as he urged the wooden horse, and lit her up, as she stood, blonde, in her dress of pale green and crystal, in the doorway.

'Paul!' she cried. 'Whatever are you doing?'

'It's Malabar!' he screamed in a powerful, strange voice. 'It's Malabar!'

His eyes blazed at her for one strange and senseless second, as he ceased urging his wooden horse. Then he fell with a crash to the ground, and she, all her tormented motherhood flooding upon her, rushed to gather him up.

But he was unconscious, and unconscious he remained, with some brain-fever. He talked and tossed, and his mother sat stonily by his side.

'Malabar! It's Malabar! Bassett, Bassett, I *know*! It's Malabar!'

So the child cried, trying to get up and urge the rocking-horse that gave him his inspiration.

'What does he mean by Malabar?' asked the heart-frozen mother.

'I don't know,' said the father stonily.

'What does he mean by Malabar?' she asked her brother Oscar.

'It's one of the horses running for the Derby,' was the answer.

And, in spite of himself, Oscar Cresswell spoke to Bassett, and himself put a thousand on Malabar: at fourteen to one.

The third day of the illness was critical: they were waiting for a change. The boy, with his rather long, curly hair, was tossing ceaselessly on the pillow. He neither slept nor regained consciousness, and his eyes were like blue stones. His mother sat, feeling her heart had gone, turned actually into a stone.

In the evening, Oscar Cresswell did not come, but Bassett sent a message, saying could he come up for one moment, just one moment? Paul's mother was very angry at the intrusion, but on second thoughts she agreed. The boy was the same. Perhaps Bassett might bring him to consciousness.

The gardener, a shortish fellow with a little brown moustache and sharp little brown eyes, tiptoed into the room, touched his imaginary cap to Paul's mother, and stole to the bedside, staring with glittering, smallish eyes at the tossing, dying child.

'Master Paul!' he whispered. 'Master Paul! Malabar came in first all right, a clean win. I did as you told me. You've made over seventy thousand pounds, you have; you've got over eighty thousand. Malabar came in all right, Master Paul.'

'Malabar! Malabar! Did I say Malabar, mother? Did I say Malabar? Do you think I'm lucky, mother? I knew Malabar, didn't I? Over eighty thousand pounds! I call that lucky, don't you, mother? Over eighty thousand pounds! I knew, didn't I know I knew? Malabar came in all right. If I ride my horse till I'm sure, then I tell you, Bassett, you can go as high as you like. Did you go for all you were worth, Bassett?'

'I went a thousand on it, Master Paul.'

'I never told you, mother, that if I can ride my horse, and *get there*, then I'm absolutely sure – oh, absolutely! Mother, did I ever tell you? I *am* lucky!'

'No, you never did,' said his mother.

But the boy died in the night.

And even as he lay dead, his mother heard her brother's voice saying to her: 'My God, Hester, you're eighty-odd thousand to the good, and a poor devil of a son to the bad. But, poor devil, poor devil, he's best gone out of a life where he rides his rocking-horse to find a winner.'

The Man who Loved Islands

I

THERE was a man who loved islands. He was born on one, but it didn't suit him, as there were too many other people on it, besides himself. He wanted an island all of his own: not necessarily to be alone on it, but to make it a world of his own.

An island, if it is big enough, is no better than a continent. It has to be really quite small, before it *feels* like an island; and this story will show how tiny it has to be, before you can presume to fill it with your own personality.

Now circumstances so worked out that this lover of islands, by the time he was thirty-five, actually acquired an island of his own. He didn't own it as freehold property, but he had a ninety-nine years' lease of it, which, as far as a man and an island are concerned, is as good as everlasting. Since, if you are like Abraham, and want your offspring to be numberless as the sands of the sea-shore, you don't choose an island to start breeding on. Too soon there would be over-population, overcrowding, and slum conditions. Which is a horrid thought, for one who loves an island for its insulation. No, an island is a nest which holds one egg, and one only. This egg is the islander himself.

The island acquired by our potential islander was not in the remote oceans. It was quite near at home, no palm trees nor boom of surf on the reef, nor any of that kind of thing; but a good solid dwelling-house, rather gloomy, above the landing-place, and beyond, a small farmhouse with sheds, and a few outlying fields. Down on the little landing-bay were three cottages in a row, like coastguards' cottages, all neat and whitewashed.

What could be more cosy and home-like? It was four miles if you walked all round your island, through the gorse and the blackthorn bushes, above the steep rocks of the sea and down in the little glades where the primroses grew. If you walked straight over the two humps of hills, the length of it, through the rocky fields where the cows lay chewing, and through the rather sparse oats, on into the gorse again, and so to the low cliffs' edge, it took you only twenty minutes. And when you came to the edge, you could see another, bigger island lying beyond. But the sea was between you and it. And as you returned over the turf where the short, downland cowslips nodded, you saw to the east still another island, a tiny one this time, like the calf of the cow. This tiny island also belonged to the islander.

Thus it seems that even islands like to keep each other company.

Our islander loved his island very much. In early spring, the little ways and glades were a snow of blackthorn, a vivid white among the Celtic stillness of close green and grey rock, blackbirds calling out in the whiteness their first long, triumphant calls. After the blackthorn and the nestling primroses came the blue apparition of hyacinths, like elfin lakes and slipping sheets of blue, among the bushes and under the glade of trees. And many birds with nests you could peep into, on the island all your own. Wonderful what a great world it was!

Followed summer, and the cowslips gone, the wild roses faintly fragrant through the haze. There was a field of hay, the foxgloves stood looking down. In a little cove, the sun was on the pale granite where you bathed, and the shadow was in the rocks. Before the mist came stealing, you went home through the ripening oats, the glare of the sea fading from the high air as the fog-horn started to moo on the other island. And then the sea-fog went, it was autumn, the oat-sheaves lying prone, the great moon, another island, rose golden out of the sea, and rising higher, the world of the sea was white.

So autumn ended with rain, and winter came, dark skies and dampness and rain, but rarely frost. The island, your island, cowered dark, holding away from you. You could feel, down in the wet, sombre hollows, the resentful spirit coiled upon itself, like a wet dog coiled in gloom, or a snake that is neither asleep nor awake. Then in the night, when the wind left off blowing in great gusts and volleys, as at sea, you felt that your island was a universe, infinite and old as the darkness; not an island at all, but an infinite dark world where all the souls from all the other bygone nights lived on, and the infinite distance was near.

Strangely, from your little island in space, you were gone forth into the dark, great realms of time, where all the souls that never die veer and swoop on their vast, strange errands. The little earthly island has dwindled, like a jumping-off place, into nothingness, for you have jumped off, you know not how, into the dark wide mystery of time, where the past is vastly alive, and the future is not separated off.

This is the danger of becoming an islander. When, in the city, you wear your white spats and dodge the traffic with the fear of death down your spine, then you are quite safe from the terrors of infinite time. The moment is your little islet in time, it is the spatial universe that careers round you.

But once isolate yourself on a little island in the sea of space, and the moment begins to heave and expand in great circles, the solid earth is gone, and your slippery, naked dark soul finds herself out in the timeless world, where the chariots of the so-called dead dash down the old streets of centuries, and souls crowd on the footways that we, in the moment, call bygone years. The souls of all the dead are alive again, and pulsating actively around you. You are out in the other infinity.

Something of this happened to our islander. Mysterious 'feelings' came upon him that he wasn't used to; strange awarenesses of old, far-gone men, and other influences; men of Gaul, with big moustaches, who had been on his island, and had vanished from the face of it, but not out of the air of night. They were there still, hurtling their big, violent, unseen bodies through the night. And there were priests, with golden knives and mistletoe; then other priests with a crucifix; then pirates with murder on the sea.

Our islander was uneasy. He didn't believe, in the day-time, in any of this nonsense. But at night it just was so. He had reduced himself to a single point in space, and, a point being that which has neither length nor breadth, he had to step off it into somewhere else. Just as you must step into the sea, if the waters wash your foothold away, so he had, at night, to step off into the other worlds of undying time.

He was uncannily aware, as he lay in the dark, that the blackthorn grove that seemed a bit uncanny even in the realm of space and day, at night was crying with old men of an invisible race, around the altar stone. What was a ruin under the hornbeam trees by day, was a moaning of blood-stained priests with crucifixes, on the ineffable night. What was a cave and a hidden beach between coarse rocks, became in the invisible dark the purple-lipped imprecation of pirates.

To escape any more of this sort of awareness, our islander daily concentrated upon his material island. Why should it not be the Happy Isle at last? Why not the last small isle of the Hesperides, the perfect place, all filled with his own gracious, blossom-like spirit? A minute world of pure perfection, made by man himself.

He began, as we begin all our attempts to regain Paradise, by spending money. The old, semi-feudal dwelling-house he restored, let in more light, put clear lovely carpets on the floor, clear, flower-petal curtains at the sullen windows, and wines in the cellars of rock. He brought over a buxom housekeeper from the world, and a soft-spoken, much-experienced butler. These two were to be islanders.

In the farmhouse he put a bailiff, with two farm-hands. There were Jersey cows, tinkling a slow bell, among the gorse. There was a call to meals at midday, and the peaceful smoking of chimneys at evening, when rest descended.

A jaunty sailing-boat with a motor accessory rode in the shelter in the bay, just below the row of three white cottages. There was also a little yawl, and two row-boats drawn up on the sand. A fishing-net was drying on its supports, a boat-load of new white planks stood criss-cross, a woman was going to the well with a bucket.

In the end cottage lived the skipper of the yacht, and his wife and son. He was a man from the other, large island, at home on this sea. Every fine day he went out fishing, with his son, every fair day there was fresh fish in the island.

In the middle cottage lived an old man and wife, a very faithful couple. The old man was a carpenter, and man of many jobs. He was always working, always the sound of his plane or his saw; lost in his work, he was another kind of islander.

In the third cottage was a mason, a widower with a son and two daughters. With the help of his boy, this man dug ditches and built fences, raised buttresses and erected a new outbuilding, and hewed stone from the little quarry. One daughter worked at the big house.

It was a quiet, busy little world. When the islander brought you over as his guest, you met first the dark-bearded, thin, smiling skipper, Arnold, then his boy Charles. At the house, the smooth-lipped butler who had lived all over the world valeted you, and created that curious creamy-smooth, disarming sense of luxury around you which only a perfect and rather untrustworthy servant can create. He disarmed you and had you at his mercy. The buxom housekeeper smiled and treated you with the subtly respectful familiarity that is only dealt out to the true gentry. And the rosy maid threw a glance at you, as if you were very wonderful, coming from the greater outer world. Then you met the smiling but watchful bailiff, who came from Cornwall, and the shy farm-hand from Berkshire, with his clean wife and two little children: then the rather sulky farm-hand from Suffolk. The mason, a Kent man, would talk to you by the yard if you let him. Only the old carpenter was gruff and elsewhere absorbed.

Well then, it was a little world to itself, and everybody feeling very safe, and being very nice to you, as if you were really something special. But it was the islander's world, not yours. He was the Master. The special smile, the special attention was to the Master. They all knew how well off they were. So the islander was no longer Mr So-and-So. To everyone on the island, even to you yourself, he was 'the Master'.

Well, it was ideal. The Master was no tyrant. Ah, no! He was a delicate, sensitive, handsome Master, who wanted everything perfect and everybody happy. Himself, of course, to be the fount of this happiness and perfection.

But in his way, he was a poet. He treated his guests royally, his servants liberally. Yet he was shrewd, and very wise. He never came the boss over his people. Yet he kept his eye on everything, like a shrewd, blue-eyed young Hermes. And it was amazing what a lot of knowledge he had at hand. Amazing what he knew about Jersey cows, and cheese-making, ditching and fencing, flowers and gardening, ships and the sailing of ships. He was a fount of knowledge about everything, and this knowledge he imparted to his people in an odd, half-ironical, half-portentous fashion, as if he really belonged to the quaint, half-real world of the gods.

They listened to him with their hats in their hands. He loved white clothes; or creamy white; and cloaks, and broad hats. So, in fine weather, the bailiff would see the elegant tall figure in creamy-white serge coming like some bird over the fallow, to look at the weeding of the turnips. Then there would be a doffing of hats, and a few minutes of whimsical, shrewd, wise talk, to which the bailiff answered admiringly, and the farm-hands listened in silent wonder, leaning on their hoes. The bailiff was almost tender, to the Master.

Or, on a windy morning, he would stand with his cloak blowing in the sticky sea-wind, on the edge of the ditch that was being dug to drain a little swamp, talking in the teeth of the wind to the man below, who looked up at him with steady and inscrutable eyes.

Or at evening in the rain he would be seen hurrying across the yard, the broad hat turned against the rain. And the farm-wife would hurriedly exclaim: 'The Master! Get up, John, and clear him a place on the sofa.' And then the door opened, and it was a cry of: 'Why, of all things, if it isn't the Master! Why, have ye turned out then, of a night like this, to come across to the like of we?' And the bailiff took his cloak, and the farm-wife his hat, the two farm-hands drew their chairs to the back, he sat on the sofa and took a child up near him. He was wonderful with children, talked to them simply wonderful, made you think of Our Saviour Himself, said the woman.

He was always greeted with smiles, and the same peculiar deference, as if he were a higher, but also frailer being. They handled him almost tenderly, and almost with adulation. But when he left, or when they spoke of him, they had often a subtle, mocking smile on their faces. There was no need to be afraid of 'the Master'. Just let him have his own way. Only the old carpenter was sometimes sincerely rude to him; so he didn't care for the old man.

It is doubtful whether any of them really liked him, man to man, or even woman to man. But then it is doubtful if he really liked any of them, as man to man, or man to woman. He wanted them to be happy, and the little world to be perfect. But anyone who wants the world to be perfect must be careful not to have real likes or dislikes. A general goodwill is all you can afford.

The sad fact is, alas, that general goodwill is always felt as something of an insult, by the mere object of it; and so it breeds a quite special brand of malice. Surely general goodwill is a form of egoism, that it should have such a result!

Our islander, however, had his own resources. He spent long hours in his library, for he was compiling a book of references to all the flowers mentioned in the Greek and Latin authors. He was not a great classical scholar; the usual public-school equipment. But there are such excellent translations nowadays. And it was so lovely, tracing flower after flower as it blossomed in the ancient world.

So the first year on the island passed by. A great deal had been done. Now the bills flooded in, and the Master, conscientious in all things, began to study them. The study left him pale and breathless. He was not a rich man. He knew he had been making a hole in his capital to get the island into running order. When he came to look, however, there was hardly anything left but hole. Thousands and thousands of pounds had the island swallowed into nothingness.

But surely the bulk of the spending was over! Surely the island would now begin to be self-supporting, even if it made no profit! Surely he was safe. He paid a good many of the bills, and took a little heart. But he had had a shock, and the next year, the coming year, there must be economy, frugality. He told his people so in simple and touching language. And they said: 'Why, surely! Surely!'

So, while the wind blew and the rain lashed outside, he would sit in his library with the bailiff over a pipe and pot of beer, discussing farm projects. He lifted his narrow, handsome face, and his blue eyes became dreamy. '*What* a wind!' It blew like cannon-shots. He thought of his island, lashed with foam, and inaccessible, and he exulted ... No, he must not lose it. He turned back to the farm projects with the zest of genius, and his hands flicked white emphasis, while the bailiff intoned: 'Yes, sir! Yes, sir! You're right, Master!'

But the man was hardly listening. He was looking at the Master's blue lawn shirt and curious pink tie with the fiery red stone, at the enamel sleeve-links, and at the ring with the peculiar scarab. The brown searching eyes of the man of the soil glanced repeatedly over the fine, immaculate figure of the Master, with a sort of slow, calculating wonder. But if he happened to catch the Master's bright, exalted glance, his own eye lit up with a careful cordiality and deference, as he bowed his head slightly.

Thus between them they decided what crops should be sown, what fertilizers should be used in different places, which breed of pigs should be imported, and which line of turkeys. That is to say, the bailiff, by continually cautiously agreeing with the Master, kept out of it, and let the young man have his own way.

The Master knew what he was talking about. He was brilliant at grasping the gist of a book, and knowing how to apply his knowledge. On the whole, his ideas were sound. The bailiff even knew it. But in the man of the soil there was no answering enthusiasm. The brown eyes smiled their cordial deference, but the thin lips never changed. The Master pursed his own flexible mouth in a boyish versatility, as he cleverly sketched in his ideas to the other man, and the bailiff made eyes of admiration, but in his heart he was not attending, he was only watching the Master as he would have watched a queer, caged animal, quite without sympathy, not implicated.

So, it was settled, and the Master rang for Elvery, the butler, to bring a sandwich. He, the Master, was pleased. The butler saw it, and came back with anchovy and ham sandwiches, and a newly opened bottle of vermouth. There was always a newly opened bottle of something.

It was the same with the mason. The Master and he discussed the drainage of a bit of land, and more pipes were ordered, more special bricks, more this, more that.

Fine weather came at last; there was a little lull in the hard work on the island. The Master went for a short cruise in his yacht. It was not really a yacht, just a little bit of a thing. They sailed along the coast of the mainland, and put in at the ports. At every port some friend turned up, the butler made elegant little meals in the cabin. Then the Master was invited to villas and hotels, his people disembarked him as if he were a prince.

And oh, how expensive it turned out! He had to telegraph to the bank for money. And he went home again to economize.

The marsh-marigolds were blazing in the little swamp where the ditches were being dug for drainage. He almost regretted, now, the work in hand. The yellow beauties would not blaze again.

Harvest came, and a bumper crop. There must be a harvest-home supper. The long barn was now completely restored and added to. The carpenter had made long tables. Lanterns hung from the beams of the high-pitched roof. All the people of the island were assembled. The bailiff presided. It was a gay scene.

Towards the end of the supper the Master, in a velvet jacket, appeared with his guests. Then the bailiff rose and proposed 'The Master! Long life and health to the Master!' All the people drank the health with great enthusiasm and cheering. The Master replied with a little speech: They were on an island in a little world of their own. It depended on them all to make this world a world of true happiness and content. Each must do his part. He hoped he himself did what he could, for his heart was in his island, and with the people of his island.

The butler responded: As long as the island had such a Master, it could not help but be a little heaven for all the people on it. This was seconded with virile warmth by the bailiff and the mason, the skipper was beside himself. Then there was dancing, the old carpenter was fiddler.

But under all this, things were not well. The very next morning came the farm-boy to say that a cow had fallen over the cliff. The Master went to look. He peered over the not very high declivity, and saw her lying dead on a green ledge under a bit of late-flowering broom. A beautiful, expensive creature, already looking swollen. But what a fool, to fall so unnecessarily!

It was a question of getting several men to haul her up the bank, and then of skinning and burying her. No one would eat the meat. How repulsive it all was!

This was symbolic of the island. As sure as the spirits rose in the human breast, with a movement of joy, an invisible hand struck malevolently out of the silence. There must not be any joy, nor even any quiet peace. A man broke a leg, another was crippled with rheumatic fever. The pigs had some strange disease. A storm drove the yacht on a rock. The mason hated the butler, and refused to let his daughter serve at the house.

Out of the very air came a stony, heavy malevolence. The island itself seemed malicious. It would go on being hurtful and evil for weeks at a time. Then suddenly again one morning it would be fair, lovely as a morning in Paradise, everything beautiful and flowing. And everybody would begin to feel a great relief, and a hope for happiness.

Then as soon as the Master was opened out in spirit like an open flower, some ugly blow would fall. Somebody would send him an anonymous note, accusing some other person on the island. Somebody else would come hinting things against one of his servants.

'Some folks think they've got an easy job out here, with

all the pickings they make!' the mason's daughter screamed at the suave butler, in the Master's hearing. He pretended not to hear.

'My man says this island is surely one of the lean kine of Egypt, it would swallow a sight of money, and you'd never get anything back out of it,' confided the farm-hand's wife to one of the Master's visitors.

The people were not contented. They were not islanders. 'We feel we're not doing right by the children,' said those who had children. 'We feel we're not doing right by ourselves,' said those who had no children. And the various families fairly came to hate one another.

Yet the island was so lovely. When there was a scent of honeysuckle and the moon brightly flickering down on the sea, then even the grumblers felt a strange nostalgia for it. It set you yearning, with a wild yearning; perhaps for the past, to be far back in the mysterious past of the island, when the blood had a different throb. Strange floods of passion came over you, strange violent lusts and imaginations of cruelty. The blood and the passion and the lust which the island had known. Uncanny dreams, half-dreams, half-evocated yearnings.

The Master himself began to be a little afraid of his island. He felt here strange, violent feelings he had never felt before, and lustful desires that he had been quite free from. He knew quite well now that his people didn't love him at all. He knew that their spirits were secretly against him, malicious, jeering, envious, and lurking to down him. He became just as wary and secretive with regard to them.

But it was too much. At the end of the second year, several departures took place. The housekeeper went. The Master always blamed self-important women most. The mason said he wasn't going to be monkeyed about any more, so he took his departure, with his family. The rheumatic farm-hand left.

And then the year's bills came in, the Master made up his accounts. In spite of good crops, the assets were ridiculous, against the spending. The island had again lost, not hundreds but thousands of pounds. It was incredible. But you simply couldn't believe it! Where had it all gone?

The Master spent gloomy nights and days going through accounts in the library. He was thorough. It became evident, now the housekeeper had gone, that she had swindled him. Probably everybody was swindling him. But he hated to think it, so he put the thought away.

He emerged, however, pale and hollow-eyed from his balancing of unbalanceable accounts, looking as if something had kicked him in the stomach. It was pitiable. But the money had gone, and there was an end of it. Another great hole in his capital. How could people be so heartless?

It couldn't go on, that was evident. He would soon be bankrupt. He had to give regretful notice to his butler. He was afraid to find out how much his butler had swindled him. Because the man was such a wonderful butler, after all. And the farm bailiff had to go. The Master had no regrets in that quarter. The losses on the farm had almost embittered him.

The third year was spent in rigid cutting down of expenses. The island was still mysterious and fascinating. But it was also treacherous and cruel, secretly, fathomlessly malevolent. In spite of all its fair show of white blossom and bluebells, and the lovely dignity of foxgloves bending their rose-red bells, it was your implacable enemy.

With reduced staff, reduced wages, reduced splendour, the third year went by. But it was fighting against hope. The farm still lost a good deal. And once more there was a hole in that remnant of capital. Another hole in that which was already a mere remnant round the old holes. The island was mysterious in this also: it seemed to pick the very money out of your pocket, as if it were an octopus with invisible arms stealing from you in every direction.

Yet the Master still loved it. But with a touch of rancour now.

He spent, however, the second half of the fourth year intensely working on the mainland, to be rid of it. And it was amazing how difficult he found it, to dispose of an island.

He had thought that everybody was pining for such an island as his; but not at all. Nobody would pay any price for it. And he wanted now to get rid of it, as a man who wants a divorce at any cost.

It was not till the middle of the fifth year that he transferred it, at a considerable loss to himself, to an hotel company who were willing to speculate in it. They were to turn it into a handy honeymoon-and-golf island.

There, take that, island which didn't know when it was well off. Now be a honeymoon-and-golf island!

2

THE SECOND ISLAND

The islander had to move. But he was not going to the mainland. Oh, no! He moved to the smaller island, which still belonged to him. And he took with him the faithful old carpenter and wife, the couple he never really cared for; also a widow and daughter, who had kept house for him the last year; also an orphan lad, to help the old man.

The small island was very small; but being a hump of rock in the sea, it was bigger than it looked. There was a little track among the rocks and bushes, winding and scrambling up and down around the islet, so that it took you twenty minutes to do the circuit. It was more than you would have expected.

Still, it was an island. The islander moved himself, with all his books, into the commonplace six-roomed house up to which you had to scramble from the rocky landing-place. There were also two joined-together cottages. The old carpenter lived in one, with his wife and the lad, the widow and daughter lived in the other.

At last all was in order. The Master's books filled two rooms. It was already autumn, Orion lifting out of the sea. And in the dark nights, the Master could see the lights on his late island, where the hotel company were entertaining guests who would advertise the new resort for honeymoon-golfers.

On his lump of rock, however, the Master was still master. He explored the crannies, the odd hand-breadths of grassy level, the steep little cliffs where the last harebells hung and the seeds of summer were brown above the sea, lonely and untouched. He peered down the old well. He examined the stone pen where the pig had been kept. Himself, he had a goat.

Yes, it was an island. Always, always underneath among the rocks the Celtic sea sucked and washed and smote its feathery greyness. How many different noises of the sea! Deep explosions, rumblings, strange long sighs and whistling noises; then voices, real voices of people clamouring as if they were in a market, under the waters: and again, the far-off ringing of a bell, surely an actual bell! Then a tremendous trilling noise, very long and alarming, and an undertone of hoarse gasping.

On this island there were no human ghosts, no ghosts of any ancient race. The sea, and the spume and the weather, had washed them all out, washed them out so there was only the sound of the sea itself, its own ghost, myriad-voiced, communing and plotting and shouting all winter long. And only the smell of the sea, with a few bristly bushes of gorse and coarse tufts of heather, among the grey, pellucid rocks, in the grey, more-pellucid air. The coldness, the greyness, even the soft, creeping fog of the sea, and the islet of rock humped up in it all, like the last point in space.

Green star Sirius stood over the sea's rim. The island was a shadow. Out at sea a ship showed small lights. Below, in the rocky cove, the row-boat and the motor-boat were safe. A light shone in the carpenter's kitchen. That was all.

Save, of course, that the lamp was lit in the house, where the widow was preparing supper, her daughter helping. The islander went in to his meal. Here he was no longer the Master, he was an islander again and he had peace. The old carpenter, the widow and daughter were all faithfulness itself. The old man worked while ever there was light to see, because he had a passion for work. The widow and her quiet, rather delicate daughter of thirty-three worked for the Master, because they loved looking after him, and they were infinitely grateful for the haven he provided them. But they didn't call him 'the Master'. They gave him his name: 'Mr Cathcart, sir!' softly and reverently. And he spoke back to them also softly, gently, like people far from the world, afraid to make a noise.

The island was no longer a 'world'. It was a sort of refuge. The islander no longer struggled for anything. He had no need. It was as if he and his few dependents were a small flock of sea-birds alighted on this rock, as they travelled through space, and keeping together without a word. The silent mystery of travelling birds.

He spent most of his day in his study. His book was coming along. The widow's daughter could type out his manuscript for him, she was not uneducated. It was the one strange sound on the island, the typewriter. But soon even its spattering fitted in with the sea's noises, and the wind's.

The months went by. The islander worked away in his study, the people of the island went quietly about their concerns. The goat had a little black kid with yellow eyes. There were mackerel in the sea. The old man went fishing in the row-boat with the lad, when the weather was calm enough; they went off in the motor-boat to the biggest island for the post. And they brought supplies, never a penny wasted. And the days went by, and the nights, without desire, without ennui.

The strange stillness from all desire was a kind of wonder to the islander. He didn't want anything. His soul at last was still in him, his spirit was like a dim-lit cave under water, where strange sea-foliage expands upon the watery atmosphere, and scarcely sways, and a mute fish shadowily slips in and slips away again. All still and soft and uncrying, yet alive as rooted seaweed is alive.

The islander said to himself: 'Is this happiness?' He said to himself: 'I am turned into a dream. I feel nothing, or I don't know what I feel. Yet it seems to me I am happy.'

Only he had to have something upon which his mental activity could work. So he spent long, silent hours in his study, working not very fast, nor very importantly, letting the writing spin softly from him as if it were drowsy gossamer. He no longer fretted whether it were good or not, what he produced. He slowly, softly spun it like gossamer, and if it were to melt away as gossamer in autumn melts, he would not mind. It was only the soft evanescence of gossamy things which now seemed to him permanent. The very mist of eternity was in them. Whereas stone buildings, cathedrals for example, seemed to him to howl with temporary resistance, knowing they must fall at last; the tension of their long endurance seemed to howl forth from them all the time.

Sometimes he went to the mainland and to the city. Then he went elegantly, dressed in the latest style, to his club. He sat in a stall at the theatre, he shopped in Bond Street. He discussed terms for publishing his book. But over his face was that gossamy look of having dropped out of the race of progress, which made the vulgar city people feel they had won it over him, and made him glad to go back to his island.

He didn't mind if he never published his book. The years were blending into a soft mist, from which nothing obtruded. Spring came. There was never a primrose on his island, but he found a winter-aconite. There were two little sprayed bushes of blackthorn, and some wind-flowers. He began to make a list of the flowers of his islet, and that was absorbing. He noted a wild currant bush and watched for the elder flowers on a stunted little tree, then for the first yellow rags of the broom, and wild roses. Bladder campion, orchids, stitchwort, celandine, he was prouder of them than if they had been people on his island. When he came across the golden saxifrage, so inconspicuous in a damp corner, he crouched over it in a trance, he knew not for how long, looking at it. Yet it was nothing to look at. As the widow's daughter found, when he showed it her.

He had said to her in real triumph:

'I found the golden saxifrage this morning.'

The name sounded splendid. She looked at him with fascinated brown eyes, in which was a hollow ache that frightened him a little.

'Did you, sir? Is it a nice flower?'

He pursed his lips and tilted his brows.

'Well – not showy exactly. I'll show it you if you like.'

'I should like to see it.'

She was so quiet, so wistful. But he sensed in her a persistency which made him uneasy. She said she was so happy: really happy. She followed him quietly, like a shadow, on the rocky track where there was never room for two people to walk side by side. He went first, and could feel her there, immediately behind him, following so submissively, gloating on him from behind.

It was a kind of pity for her which made him become her lover: though he never realized the extent of the power she had gained over him, and how *she* willed it. But the moment he had fallen, a jangling feeling came upon him, that it was all wrong. He felt a nervous dislike of her. He had not wanted it. And it seemed to him, as far as her physical self went, she had not wanted it either. It was just her will. He went away, and climbed at the risk of his neck down to a ledge near the sea. There he sat for hours, gazing all jangled at the sea, and saying miserably to himself: 'We didn't want it. We didn't really want it.'

It was the automatism of sex that had caught him again. Not that he hated sex. He deemed it, as the Chinese do, one of the great life-mysteries. But it had become mechanical, automatic, and he wanted to escape that. Automatic sex shattered him, and filled him with a sort of death. He thought he had come through, to a new stillness of desirelessness. Perhaps beyond that there was a new fresh delicacy of desire, an unentered frail communion of two people meeting on untrodden ground.

Be that as it might, this was not it. This was nothing new or fresh. It was automatic, and driven from the will. Even she, in her true self, hadn't wanted it. It was automatic in her.

When he came home, very late, and saw her face white with fear and apprehension of his feeling against her, he pitied her, and spoke to her delicately, reassuringly. But he kept himself remote from her.

She gave no sign. She served him with the same silence, the

same hidden hunger to serve him, to be near where he was. He felt her love following him with strange, awful persistency. She claimed nothing. Yet now, when he met her bright, brown, curiously vacant eyes, he saw in them the mute question. The question came direct at him, with a force and a power of will he never realized.

So he succumbed, and asked her again.

'Not,' she said, 'if it will make you hate me.'

'Why should it?' he replied, nettled. 'Of course not.'

'You know I would do anything on earth for you.'

It was only afterwards, in his exasperation, he remembered what she said, and was more exasperated. Why should she pretend to do this *for him*? Why not herself? But in his exasperation, he drove himself deeper in. In order to achieve some sort of satisfaction, which he never did achieve, he abandoned himself to her. Everybody on the island knew. But he did not care.

Then even what desire he had left him, and he felt only shattered. He felt that only with her will had she wanted him. Now he was shattered and full of self-contempt. His island was smirched and spoiled. He had lost his place in the rare, desireless levels of Time to which he had at last arrived, and he had fallen right back. If only it had been true, delicate desire between them, and a delicate meeting on the third rare place where a man might meet a woman, when they were both true to the frail, sensitive, crocus-flame of desire in them. But it had been no such thing: automatic, an act of will, not of true desire, it left him feeling humiliated.

He went away from the islet, in spite of her mute reproach. And he wandered about the continent, vainly seeking a place where he could stay. He was out of key; he did not fit in the world any more.

There came a letter from Flora – her name was Flora – to say she was afraid she was going to have a child. He sat down as if he were shot, and he remained sitting. But he replied to her: 'Why be afraid? If it is so, it is so, and we should rather be pleased than afraid.'

At this very moment, it happened there was an auction of

islands. He got the maps, and studied them. And at the auction he bought, for very little money, another island. It was just a few acres of rock away in the north, on the outer fringe of the isles. It was low, it rose low out of the great ocean. There was not a building, not even a tree on it. Only northern sea-turf, a pool of rain-water, a bit of sedge, rock, and sea-birds. Nothing else. Under the weeping wet western sky.

He made a trip to visit his new possession. For several days, owing to the seas, he could not approach it. Then, in a light sea-mist, he landed, and saw it hazy, low, stretching apparently a long way. But it was illusion. He walked over the wet, springy turf, and dark-grey sheep tossed away from him, spectral, bleating hoarsely. And he came to the dark pool, with the sedge. Then on in the dampness, to the grey sea sucking angrily among the rocks.

This was indeed an island.

So he went home to Flora. She looked at him with guilty fear, but also with a triumphant brightness in her uncanny eyes. And again he was gentle, he reassured her, even he wanted her again, with that curious desire that was almost like toothache. So he took her to the mainland, and they were married, since she was going to have his child.

They returned to the island. She still brought in his meals, her own along with them. She sat and ate with him. He would have it so. The widowed mother preferred to stay in the kitchen. And Flora slept in the guest-room of his house, mistress of his house.

His desire, whatever it was, died in him with nauseous finality. The child would still be months coming. His island was hateful to him, vulgar, a suburb. He himself had lost all his finer distinction. The weeks passed in a sort of prison, in humiliation. Yet he stuck it out, till the child was born. But he was meditating escape. Flora did not even know.

A nurse appeared, and ate at table with them. The doctor came sometimes, and, if the sea were rough, he too had to stay. He was cheery over his whisky.

They might have been a young couple in Golders Green.

The daughter was born at last. The father looked at the

baby, and felt depressed, almost more than he could bear. The millstone was tied round his neck. But he tried not to show what he felt. And Flora did not know. She still smiled with a kind of half-witted triumph in her joy, as she got well again. Then she began again to look at him with those aching, suggestive, somehow impudent eyes. She adored him so.

This he could not stand. He told her that he had to go away for a time. She wept, but she thought she had got him. He told her he had settled the best part of his property on her, and wrote down for her what income it would produce. She hardly listened, only looked at him with those heavy, adoring, impudent eyes. He gave her a cheque-book, with the amount of her credit duly entered. This did arouse her interest. And he told her, if she got tired of the island, she could choose her home wherever she wished.

She followed him with those aching, persistent brown eyes, when he left, and he never even saw her weep.

He went straight north, to prepare his third island.

3

THE THIRD ISLAND

The third island was soon made habitable. With cement and the big pebbles from the shingle beach, two men built him a hut, and roofed it with corrugated iron. A boat brought over a bed and table, and three chairs, with a good cupboard, and a few books. He laid in a supply of coal and paraffin and food – he wanted so little.

The house stood near the flat shingle bay where he landed, and where he pulled up his light boat. On a sunny day in August the men sailed away and left him. The sea was still and pale blue. On the horizon he saw the small mail-steamer slowly passing northwards, as if she were walking. She served the outer isles twice a week. He could row out to her if need be, in calm weather, and he could signal her from a flagstaff behind his cottage.

Half a dozen sheep still remained on the island, as company; and he had a cat to rub against his legs. While the sweet, sunny days of the northern autumn lasted, he would walk among the rocks, and over the springy turf of his small domain, always coming to the ceaseless, restless sea. He looked at every leaf, that might be different from another, and he watched the endless expansion and contraction of the water-tossed seaweed. He had never a tree, not even a bit of heather to guard. Only the turf, and tiny turf-plants, and the sedge by the pool, the seaweed in the ocean. He was glad. He didn't want trees or bushes. They stood up like people, too assertive. His bare, low-pitched island in the pale blue sea was all he wanted.

He no longer worked at his book. The interest had gone. He liked to sit on the low elevation of his island, and see the sea; nothing but the pale, quiet sea. And to feel his mind turn soft and hazy, like the hazy ocean. Sometimes, like a mirage, he would see the shadow of land rise hovering to northwards. It was a big island beyond. But quite without substance.

He was soon almost startled when he perceived the steamer on the near horizon, and his heart contracted with fear, lest it were going to pause and molest him. Anxiously he watched it go, and not till it was out of sight did he feel truly relieved, himself again. The tension of waiting for human approach was cruel. He did not want to be approached. He did not want to hear voices. He was shocked by the sound of his own voice, if he inadvertently spoke to his cat. He rebuked himself for having broken the great silence. And he was irritated when his cat would look up at him and mew faintly, plaintively. He frowned at her. And she knew. She was becoming wild, lurking in the rocks, perhaps fishing.

But what he disliked most was when one of the lumps of sheep opened its mouth and baa-ed its hoarse, raucous baa. He watched it, and it looked to him hideous and gross. He came to dislike the sheep very much.

He wanted only to hear the whispering sound of the sea, and the sharp cries of the gulls, cries that came out of another world to him. And best of all, the great silence.

He decided to get rid of the sheep when the boat came. They

were accustomed to him now, and stood and stared at him with yellow or colourless eyes, in an insolence that was almost cold ridicule. There was a suggestion of cold indecency about them. He disliked them very much. And when they jumped with staccato jumps off the rocks, and their hoofs made the dry, sharp hit, and the fleece flopped on their square backs, he found them repulsive, degrading.

The fine weather passed, and it rained all day. He lay a great deal on his bed, listening to the water trickling from his roof into the zinc water-butt, looking through the open door at the rain, the dark rocks, the hidden sea. Many gulls were on the island now: many sea-birds of all sorts. It was another world of life. Many of the birds he had never seen before. His old impulse came over him, to send for a book, to know their names. In a flicker of the old passion, to know the name of everything he saw, he even decided to row out to the steamer. The names of these birds! He must know their names, otherwise he had not got them, they were not quite alive to him.

But the desire left him, and he merely watched the birds as they wheeled or walked around him, watched them vaguely, without discrimination. All interest had left him. Only there was one gull, a big, handsome fellow, who would walk back and forth, back and forth in front of the open door of the cabin, as if he had some mission there. He was big, and pearl-grey, and his roundnesses were as smooth and lovely as a pearl. Only the folded wings had shut black pinions, and on the closed black feathers were three distinct white dots, making a pattern. The islander wondered very much, why this bit of trimming on the bird out of the far, cold seas. And as the gull walked back and forth, back and forth in front of the cabin, strutting on pale-dusky gold feet, holding up his pale yellow beak, that was curved at the tip, with curious alien importance, the man wondered over him. He was portentous, he had a meaning.

Then the bird came no more. The island, which had been full of sea-birds, the flash of wings, the sound and cut of wings and sharp eerie cries in the air, began to be deserted again. No longer they sat like living eggs on the rocks and turf, moving their heads, but scarcely rising into flight round his feet. No longer they ran across the turf among the sheep, and lifted themselves upon low wings. The host had gone. But some remained, always.

The days shortened, and the world grew eerie. One day the boat came: as if suddenly, swooping down. The islander found it a violation. It was torture to talk to those two men, in their homely clumsy clothes. The air of familiarity around them was very repugnant to him. Himself, he was neatly dressed, his cabin was neat and tidy. He resented any intrusion, the clumsy homeliness, the heavy-footedness of the two fishermen was really repulsive to him.

The letters they had brought he left lying unopened in a little box. In one of them was his money. But he could not bear to open even that one. Any kind of contact was repulsive to him. Even to read his name on an envelope. He hid the letters away.

And the hustle and horror of getting the sheep caught and tied and put in the ship made him loathe with profound repulsion the whole of the animal creation. What repulsive god invented animals and evil-smelling men? To his nostrils, the fishermen and the sheep alike smelled foul: an uncleanness on the fresh earth.

He was still nerve-racked and tortured when the ship at last lifted sail and was drawing away, over the still sea. And sometimes, days after, he would start with repulsion, thinking he heard the munching of sheep.

The dark days of winter drew on. Sometimes there was no real day at all. He felt ill, as if he were dissolving, as if dissolution had already set in inside him. Everything was twilight, outside, and in his mind and soul. Once, when he went to the door, he saw black heads of men swimming in his bay. For some moments he swooned unconscious. It was the shock, the horror of unexpected human approach. The horror in the twilight! And not till the shock had undermined him and left him disembodied, did he realize that the black heads were the heads of seals swimming in. A sick relief came over him. But he was barely conscious, after the shock. Later on, he sat and wept with gratitude, because they were not men. But he never realized that he wept. He was too dim. Like some strange, ethereal animal, he no longer realized what he was doing.

Only he still derived his single satisfaction from being alone, absolutely alone, with the space soaking into him. The grey sea alone, and the footing of his sea-washed island. No other contact. Nothing human to bring its horror into contact with him. Only space, damp, twilit, sea-washed space! This was the bread of his soul.

For this reason, he was most glad when there was a storm, or when the sea was high. Then nothing could get at him. Nothing could come through to him from the outer world. True, the terrific violence of the wind made him suffer badly. At the same time, it swept the world utterly out of existence for him. He always liked the sea to be heavily rolling and tearing. Then no boat could get at him. It was like eternal ramparts round his island.

He kept no track of time, and no longer thought of opening a book. The print, the printed letters, so like the depravity of speech, looked obscene. He tore the brass label from his paraffin stove. He obliterated any bit of lettering in his cabin.

His cat had disappeared. He was rather glad. He shivered at her thin, obtrusive call. She had lived in the coal-shed. And each morning he had put her a dish of porridge, the same as he ate. He washed her saucer with repulsion. He did not like her writhing about. But he fed her scrupulously. Then one day she did not come for her porridge; she always mewed for it. She did not come again.

He prowled about his island in the rain, in a big oilskin coat, not knowing what he was looking at, nor what he went out to see. Time had ceased to pass. He stood for long spaces, gazing from a white, sharp face, with those keen, far-off blue eyes of his, gazing fiercely and almost cruelly at the dark sea under the dark sky. And if he saw the labouring sail of a fishing-boat away on the cold waters, a strange malevolent anger passed over his features.

Sometimes he was ill. He knew he was ill, because he staggered as he walked, and easily fell down. Then he paused to think what it was. And he went to his stores and took out dried milk and malt, and ate that. Then he forgot again. He ceased to register his own feelings.

The days were beginning to lengthen. All winter the weather had been comparatively mild, but with much rain, much rain. He had forgotten the sun. Suddenly, however, the air was very cold, and he began to shiver. A fear came over him. The sky was level and grey, and never a star appeared at night. It was very cold. More birds began to arrive. The island was freezing. With trembling hands he made a fire in his grate. The cold frightened him.

And now it continued, day after day, a dull, deathly cold. Occasional crumblings of snow were in the air. The days were greyly longer, but no change in the cold. Frozen grey daylight. The birds passed away, flying away. Some he saw lying frozen. It was as if all life were drawing away, contracting away from the north, contracting southwards. 'Soon,' he said to himself, 'it will all be gone, and in all these regions nothing will be alive.' He felt a cruel satisfaction in the thought.

Then one night there seemed to be a relief; he slept better, did not tremble half-awake, and writhe so much, half-conscious. He had become so used to the quaking and writhing of his body, he hardly noticed it. But when for once it slept deep, he noticed that.

He woke in the morning to a curious whiteness. His window was muffled. It had snowed. He got up and opened his door, and shuddered. Ugh! How cold! All white, with a dark leaden sea, and black rocks curiously speckled with white. The foam was no longer pure. It seemed dirty. And the sea ate at the whiteness of the corpse-like land. Crumbles of snow were silting down the dead air.

On the ground the snow was a foot deep, white and smooth and soft, windless. He took a shovel to clear round his house and shed. The pallor of morning darkened. There was a strange rumbling of far-off thunder in the frozen air, and through the newly-falling snow, a dim flash of lightning. Snow now fell steadily down in the motionless obscurity.

He went out for a few minutes. But it was difficult. He

stumbled and fell in the snow, which burned his face. Weak, faint, he toiled home. And when he recovered, took the trouble to make hot milk.

It snowed all the time. In the afternoon again there was a muffled rumbling of thunder, and flashes of lightning blinking reddish through the falling snow. Uneasy, he went to bed and lay staring fixedly at nothingness.

Morning seemed never to come. An eternity long he lay and waited for one alleviating pallor on the night. And at last it seemed the air was paler. His house was a cell faintly illuminated with white light. He realized the snow was walled outside his window. He got up, in the dead cold. When he opened his door, the motionless snow stopped him in a wall as high as his breast. Looking over the top of it, he felt the dead wind slowly driving, saw the snow-powder lift and travel like a funeral train. The blackish sea churned and champed, seeming to bite at the snow, impotent. The sky was grey, but luminous.

He began to work in a frenzy, to get at his boat. If he was to be shut in, it must be by his own choice, not by the mechanical power of the elements. He must get to the sea. He must be able to get at his boat.

But he was weak, and at times the snow overcame him. It fell on him, and he lay buried and lifeless. Yet every time he struggled alive before it was too late, and fell upon the snow with the energy of fever. Exhausted, he would not give in. He crept indoors and made coffee and bacon. Long since he had cooked so much. Then he went at the snow once more. He must conquer the snow, this new, white brute force which had accumulated against him.

He worked in the awful, dead wind, pushing the snow aside, pressing it with his shovel. It was cold, freezing hard in the wind, even when the sun came out for a while, and showed him his white, lifeless surroundings, the black sea rolling sullen, flecked with dull spume, away to the horizons. Yet the sun had power on his face. It was March.

He reached the boat. He pushed the snow away, then sat down under the lee of the boat, looking at the sea, which swirled nearly to his feet, in the high tide. Curiously natural the pebbles looked, in a world gone all uncanny. The sun shone no more. Snow was falling in hard crumbs, that vanished as if by a miracle as they touched the hard blackness of the sea. Hoarse waves rang in the shingle, rushing up at the snow. The wet rocks were brutally black. And all the time the myriad swooping crumbs of snow, demonish, touched the dark sea and disappeared.

During the night there was a great storm. It seemed to him he could hear the vast mass of snow striking all the world with a ceaseless thud; and over it all, the wind roared in strange hollow volleys, in between which came a jump of blindfold lightning, then the low roll of thunder heavier than the wind. When at last the dawn faintly discoloured the dark, the storm had more or less subsided, but a steady wind drove on. The snow was up to the top of his door.

Sullenly, he worked to dig himself out. And he managed through sheer persistency to get out. He was in the tail of a great drift, many feet high. When he got through, the frozen snow was not more than two feet deep. But his island was gone. Its shape was all changed, great heaping white hills rose where no hills had been, inaccessible, and they fumed like volcanoes, but with snow powder. He was sickened and overcome.

His boat was in another, smaller drift. But he had not the strength to clear it. He looked at it helplessly. The shovel slipped from his hands, and he sank in the snow, to forget. In the snow itself, the sea resounded.

Something brought him to. He crept to his house. He was almost without feeling. Yet he managed to warm himself, just that part of him which leaned in snow-sleep over the coal fire. Then again he made hot milk. After which, carefully, he built up the fire.

The wind dropped. Was it night again? In the silence, it seemed he could hear the panther-like dropping of infinite snow. Thunder rumbled nearer, crackled quick after the bleared reddened lightning. He lay in bed in a kind of stupor. The elements! The elements! His mind repeated the word dumbly. You can't win against the elements.

How long it went on, he never knew. Once, like a wraith, he got out and climbed to the top of a white hill on his unrecognizable island. The sun was hot. 'It is summer,' he said to himself, 'and the time of leaves.' He looked stupidly over the whiteness of his foreign island, over the waste of the lifeless sea. He pretended to imagine he saw the wink of a sail. Because he knew too well there would never again be a sail on that stark sea.

As he looked, the sky mysteriously darkened and chilled. From far off came the mutter of the unsatisfied thunder, and he knew it was the signal of the snow rolling over the sea. He turned, and felt its breath on him.

The Man who Died

THERE was a peasant near Jerusalem who acquired a young gamecock which looked a shabby little thing, but which put on brave feathers as spring advanced, and was resplendent with arched and orange neck by the time the fig trees were letting out leaves from their end-tips.

This peasant was poor, he lived in a cottage of mud-brick, and had only a dirty little inner courtyard with a tough fig tree for all his territory. He worked hard among the vines and olives and wheat of his master, then came home to sleep in the mud-brick cottage by the path. But he was proud of his young rooster. In the shut-in yard were three shabby hens which laid small eggs, shed the few feathers they had, and made a disproportionate amount of dirt. There was also, in a corner under a straw roof, a dull donkey that often went out with the peasant to work, but sometimes stayed at home. And there was the peasant's wife, a black-browed youngish woman who did not work too hard. She threw a little grain, or the remains of the porridge mess, to the fowls, and she cut green fodder with a sickle for the ass.

The young cock grew to a certain splendour. By some freak of destiny, he was a dandy rooster, in that dirty little yard with three patchy hens. He learned to crane his neck and give shrill answers to the crowing of other cocks, beyond the walls, in a world he knew nothing of. But there was a special fiery colour to his crow, and the distant calling of the other cocks roused him to unexpected outbursts.

'How he sings,' said the peasant, as he got up and pulled his day-shirt over his head.

'He is good for twenty hens,' said the wife.

The peasant went out and looked with pride at his young rooster. A saucy, flamboyant bird, that had already made the final acquaintance of the three tattered hens. But the cockerel was tipping his head, listening to the challenge of far-off unseen cocks, in the unknown world. Ghost voices, crowing at him mysteriously out of limbo. He answered with a ringing defiance, never to be daunted.

'He will surely fly away one of these days,' said the peasant's wife.

So they lured him with grain, caught him, though he fought with all his wings and feet, and they tied a cord round his shank, fastening it against the spur; and they tied the other end of the cord to the post that held up the donkey's straw pent-roof.

The young cock, freed, marched with a prancing stride of indignation away from the humans, came to the end of his string, gave a tug and a hitch of his tied leg, fell over for a moment, scuffled frantically on the unclean earthen floor, to the horror of the shabby hens, then with a sickening lurch, regained his feet, and stood to think. The peasant and the peasant's wife laughed heartily, and the young cock heard them. And he knew, with a gloomy, foreboding kind of knowledge that he was tied by the leg.

He no longer pranced and ruffled and forged his feathers. He walked within the limits of his tether sombrely. Still he gobbled up the best bits of food. Still, sometimes, he saved an extra-best bit for his favourite hen of the moment. Still he pranced with quivering, rocking fierceness upon such of his harem as came nonchalantly within range, and gave off the invisible lure. And still he crowed defiance to the cock-crows that showered up out of limbo, in the dawn.

But there was now a grim voracity in the way he gobbled his food, and a pinched triumph in the way he seized upon the shabby hens. His voice, above all, had lost the full gold of its clangour. He was tied by the leg, and he knew it. Body, soul, and spirit were tied by that string.

Underneath, however, the life in him was grimly unbroken. It was the cord that should break. So one morning, just before the light of dawn, rousing from his slumbers with a sudden wave of strength, he leaped forward on his wings, and the string snapped. He gave a wild, strange squawk, rose in one lift to the top of the wall, and there he crowed a loud and splitting crow. So loud, it woke the peasant.

At the same time, at the same hour before dawn, on the same morning, a man awoke from a long sleep in which he was tied up. He woke numb and cold, inside a carved hole in the rock. Through all the long sleep his body had been full of hurt, and it was still full of hurt. He did not open his eyes. Yet he knew that he was awake, and numb, and cold, and rigid, and full of hurt, and tied up. His face was banded with cold bands, his legs were bandaged together. Only his hands were loose.

He could move if he wanted: he knew that. But he had no want. Who would want to come back from the dead? A deep, deep nausea stirred in him, at the premonition of movement. He resented already the fact of the strange, incalculable moving that had already taken place in him: the moving back into consciousness. He had not wished it. He had wanted to stay outside, in the place where even memory is stone dead.

But now, something had returned to him, like a returned letter, and in that return he lay overcome with a sense of nausea. Yet suddenly his hands moved. They lifted up, cold, heavy and sore. Yet they lifted up, to drag away the cloth from his face, and push at the shoulder-bands. Then they fell again, cold, heavy, numb, and sick with having moved even so much, unspeakably unwilling to move further.

With his face cleared and his shoulders free, he lapsed again, and lay dead, resting on the cold nullity of being dead. It was the most desirable. And almost, he had it complete: the utter cold nullity of being outside.

Yet when he was most nearly gone, suddenly, driven by an ache at the wrists, his hands rose and began pushing at the bandages of his knees, his feet began to stir, even while his breast lay cold and dead still.

And at last, the eyes opened. On to the dark. The same dark! Yet perhaps there was a pale chink, of the all-disturbing light, prising open the pure dark. He could not lift his head. The eyes closed. And again it was finished.

Then suddenly he leaned up, and the great world reeled.

Bandages fell away. And narrow walls of rock closed upon him, and gave the new anguish of imprisonment. There were chinks of light. With a wave of strength that came from revulsion, he leaned forward, in that narrow well of rock, and leaned frail hands on the rock near the chinks of light.

Strength came from somewhere, from revulsion; there was a crash and a wave of light, and the dead man was crouching in his lair, facing the animal onrush of light. Yet it was hardly dawn. And the strange, piercing keenness of daybreak's sharp breath was on him. It meant full awakening.

Slowly, slowly he crept down from the cell of rock with the caution of the bitterly wounded. Bandages and linen and perfume fell away, and he crouched on the ground against the wall of rock, to recover oblivion. But he saw his hurt feet touching the earth again, with unspeakable pain, the earth they had meant to touch no more, and he saw his thin legs that had died, and pain unknowable, pain like utter bodily disillusion, filled him so full that he stood up, with one torn hand on the ledge of the tomb.

To be back! To be back again, after all that! He saw the linen swathing-bands fallen round his dead feet, and stooping, he picked them up, folded them, and laid them back in the rocky cavity from which he had emerged. Then he took the perfumed linen sheet, wrapped it round him as a mantle, and turned away, to the wanness of the chill dawn.

He was alone; and having died, was even beyond loneliness.

Filled still with the sickness of unspeakable disillusion, the man stepped with wincing feet down the rocky slope, past the sleeping soldiers, who lay wrapped in their woollen mantles under the wild laurels. Silent, on naked scarred feet, wrapped in a white linen shroud, he glanced down for a moment on the inert, heap-like bodies of the soldiers. They were repulsive, a slow squalor of limbs, yet he felt a certain compassion. He passed on towards the road, lest they should wake.

Having nowhere to go, he turned from the city that stood on her hills. He slowly followed the road away from the town, past the olives, under which purple anemones were drooping in the chill of dawn, and rich-green herbage was pressing thick. The world, the same as ever, the natural world, thronging with greenness, a nightingale winsomely, wistfully, coaxingly calling from the bushes beside a runnel of water, in the world, the natural world of morning and evening, for ever undying, from which he had died.

He went on, on scarred feet, neither of this world nor of the next. Neither here nor there, neither seeing nor yet sightless, he passed dimly on, away from the city and its precincts, wondering why he should be travelling, yet driven by a dim, deep nausea of disillusion, and a resolution of which he was not even aware.

Advancing in a kind of half-consciousness under the dry stone wall of the olive orchard, he was roused by the shrill, wild crowing of a cock just near him, a sound which made him shiver, as if electricity had touched him. He saw a black and orange cock on a bough above the road, then running through the olives of the upper level, a peasant in a grey woollen shirt-tunic. Leaping out of greenness, came the black and orange cock with the red comb, his tail-feathers streaming lustrous.

'O, stop him, master!' called the peasant. 'My escaped cock!'

The man addressed, with a sudden flicker of smile, opened his great white wings of a shroud in front of the leaping bird. The cock fell back with a squawk and a flutter, the peasant jumped forward, there was a terrific beating of wings and whirring of feathers, then the peasant had the escaped cock safely under his arm, its wings shut down, its face crazily craning forward, its round eyes goggling from its white chops.

'It's my escaped cock!' said the peasant, soothing the bird with his left hand, as he looked perspiringly up into the face of the man wrapped in white linen.

The peasant changed countenance, and stood transfixed, as he looked into the dead-white face of the man who had died. That dead-white face, so still, with the black beard growing on it as if in death; and those wide-open, black, sombre eyes, that had died! and those washed scars on the waxy forehead!

The slow-blooded man of the field let his jaw drop, in childish inability to meet the situation.

'Don't be afraid,' said the man in the shroud. 'I am not dead. They took me down too soon. So I have risen up. Yet if they discover me, they will do it all over again . . .'

He spoke in a voice of old disgust. Humanity! Especially humanity, in authority! There was only one thing it could do! He looked with black, indifferent eyes into the quick, shifty eyes of the peasant. The peasant quailed, and was powerless under the look of deathly indifference and strange, cold resoluteness. He could only say the one thing he was afraid to say:

'Will you hide in my house, master?'

'I will rest there. But if you tell anyone, you know what will happen. You will have to go before a judge.'

'Me! I shan't speak. Let us be quick!'

The peasant looked round in fear, wondering sulkily why he had let himself in for this doom. The man with scarred feet climbed painfully up to the level of the olive garden, and followed the sullen, hurrying peasant across the green wheat among the olive trees. He felt the cool silkiness of the young wheat under his feet that had been dead, and the roughishness of its separate life was apparent to him. At the edges of rocks, he saw the silky, silvery-haired buds of the scarlet anemone bending downwards. And they, too, were in another world. In his own world he was alone, utterly alone. These things around him were in a world that had never died. But he himself had died, or had been killed from out of it, and all that remained now was the great void nausea of utter disillusion.

They came to a clay cottage, and the peasant waited dejectedly for the other man to pass.

'Pass!' he said. 'Pass! We have not been seen.'

The man in white linen entered the earthen room, taking with him the aroma of strange perfumes. The peasant closed the door, and passed through the inner doorway into the yard, where the ass stood within the high walls, safe from being stolen. There the peasant, in great disquietude, tied up the cock. The man with the waxen face sat down on a mat near the hearth, for he was spent and barely conscious. Yet he heard outside the whispering of the peasant to his wife, for the woman had been watching from the roof.

Presently they came in, and the woman hid her face. She poured water, and put bread and dried figs on a wooden platter.

'Eat, master!' said the peasant. 'Eat! No one has seen.'

But the stranger had no desire for food. Yet he moistened a little bread in the water, and ate it, since life must be. But desire was dead in him, even for food and drink. He had risen without desire, without even the desire to live, empty save for the all-overwhelming disillusion that lay like nausea where his life had been. Yet perhaps, deeper even than disillusion, was a desireless resoluteness, deeper even than consciousness.

The peasant and his wife stood near the door, watching. They saw with terror the livid wounds on the thin, waxy hands and the thin feet of the stranger, and the small lacerations in the still dead forehead. They smelled with terror the scent of rich perfumes that came from him, from his body. And they looked at the fine, snowy, costly linen. Perhaps really he was a dead king, from the region of terrors. And he was still cold and remote in the region of death, with perfumes coming from his transparent body as if from some strange flower.

Having with difficulty swallowed some of the moistened bread, he lifted his eyes to them. He saw them as they were: limited, meagre in their life, without any splendour of gesture and of courage. But they were what they were, slow, inevitable parts of the natural world. They had no nobility, but fear made them compassionate.

And the stranger had compassion on them again, for he knew that they would respond best to gentleness, giving back a clumsy gentleness again.

'Do not be afraid,' he said to them gently. 'Let me stay a little while with you. I shall not stay long. And then I shall go away for ever. But do not be afraid. No harm will come to you through me.'

They believed him at once, yet the fear did not leave them. And they said:

'Stay, master, while ever you will. Rest! Rest quietly!'

131

But they were afraid.

So he let them be, and the peasant went away with the ass. The sun had risen bright, and in the dark house with the door shut, the man was again as if in the tomb. So he said to the woman: 'I would lie in the yard.'

And she swept the yard for him, and laid him a mat, and he lay down under the wall in the morning sun. There he saw the first green leaves spurting like flames from the ends of the enclosed fig tree, out of the bareness to the sky of spring above. But the man who had died could not look, he only lay quite still in the sun, which was not yet too hot, and had no desire in him, not even to move. But he lay with his thin legs in the sun, his black, perfumed hair falling into the hollows of his neck, and his thin, colourless arms utterly inert. As he lay there, the hens clucked, and scratched, and the escaped cock, caught and tied by the leg again, cowered in a corner.

The peasant woman was frightened. She came peeping, and, seeing him never move, feared to have a dead man in the yard. But the sun had grown stronger, he opened his eyes and looked at her. And now she was frightened of the man who was alive but spoke nothing.

He opened his eyes, and saw the world again bright as glass. It was life, in which he had no share any more. But it shone outside him, blue sky, and a bare fig tree with little jets of green leaf. Bright as glass, and he was not of it, for desire had failed.

Yet he was there, and not extinguished. The day passed in a kind of coma, and at evening he went into the house. The peasant man came home, but he was frightened, and had nothing to say. The stranger, too, ate of the mess of beans, a little. Then he washed his hands and turned to the wall, and was silent. The peasants were silent too. They watched their guest sleep. Sleep was so near death he could still sleep.

Yet when the sun came up, he went again to lie in the yard. The sun was the one thing that drew him and swayed him, and he still wanted to feel the cool air of the morning in his nostrils, see the pale sky overhead. He still hated to be shut up.

As he came out, the young cock crowed. It was a diminished,

pinched cry, but there was that in the voice of the bird stronger
than chagrin. It was the necessity to live, and even to
cry out the triumph of life. The man who had died stood
and watched the cock who had escaped and been caught,
ruffling himself up, rising forward on his toes, throwing up
his head, and parting his beak in another challenge from life
to death. The brave sounds rang out, and though they were
diminished by the cord round the bird's leg, they were not cut
off. The man who had died looked nakedly on life, and saw a
vast resoluteness everywhere flinging itself up in stormy or
subtle wave-crests, foam-tips emerging out of the blue invisible, a black and orange cock or the green flame-tongues
out of the extremes of the fig tree. They came forth, these
things and creatures of spring, glowing with desire and with
assertion. They came like crests of foam, out of the blue flood
of the invisible desire, out of the vast invisible sea of strength,
and they came coloured and tangible, evanescent, yet deathless
in their coming. The man who had died looked on the great
swing into existence of things that had not died, but he saw no
longer their tremulous desire to exist and to be. He heard
instead their ringing, ringing, defiant challenge to all other
things existing.

The man lay still, with eyes that had died now wide open
and darkly still, seeing the everlasting resoluteness of life. And
the cock, with the flat, brilliant glance, glanced back at him,
with a bird's half-seeing look. And always the man who had
died saw not the bird alone, but the short, sharp wave of life of
which the bird was the crest. He watched the queer, beaky
motion of the creature as it gobbled into itself the scraps of
food; its glancing of the eye of life, ever alert and watchful,
over-weening and cautious, and the voice of its life, crowing
triumph and assertion, yet strangled by a cord of circumstance.
He seemed to hear the queer speech of very life, as the cock
triumphantly imitated the clucking of the favourite hen, when
she had laid an egg, a clucking which still had, in the male
bird, the hollow chagrin of the cord round his leg. And when
the man threw a bit of bread to the cock, it called with an
extraordinary cooing tenderness, tousling and saving the

morsel for the hens. The hens ran up greedily, and carried the morsel away beyond the reach of the string.

Then, walking complacently after them, suddenly the male bird's leg would hitch at the end of his tether, and he would yield with a kind of collapse. His flag fell, he seemed to diminish, he would huddle in the shade. And he was young, his tail-feathers, glossy as they were, were not fully grown. It was not till evening again that the tide of life in him made him forget. Then when his favourite hen came strolling unconcernedly near him, emitting the lure, he pounced on her with all his feathers vibrating. And the man who had died watched the unsteady, rocking vibration of the bent bird, and it was not the bird he saw, but one wave-tip of life overlapping for a minute another, in the tide of the swaying ocean of life. And the destiny of life seemed more fierce and compulsive to him even than the destiny of death. The doom of death was a shadow compared to the raging destiny of life, the determined surge of life.

At twilight the peasant came home with the ass, and he said: 'Master! It is said that the body was stolen from the garden, and the tomb is empty, and the soldiers are taken away, accursed Romans! And the women are there to weep.'

The man who had died looked at the man who had not died.

'It is well,' he said. 'Say nothing, and we are safe.'

And the peasant was relieved He looked rather dirty and stupid, and even as much flaminess as that of the young cock, which he had tied by the leg, would never glow in him. He was without fire. But the man who had died thought to himself:

'Why, then, should he be lifted up? Clods of earth are turned over for refreshment, they are not to be lifted up. Let the earth remain earthy, and hold its own again the sky. I was to seek to lift it up. I was wrong to try to interfere. The ploughshare of devastation will be set in the soil of Judea, and the life of this peasant will be overturned like the sods of the field. No man can save the earth from tillage. It is tillage, not salvation . . .'

So he saw the man, the peasant, with compassion; but the

man who had died no longer wished to interfere in the soul of the man who had not died, and who could never die, save to return to earth. Let him return to earth in his own good hour, and let no one try to interfere when the earth claims her own.

So the man with scars let the peasant go from him, for the peasant had no rebirth in him. Yet the man who had died said to himself: 'He is my host.'

And at dawn, when he was better, the man who had died rose up, and on slow, sore feet retraced his way to the garden. For he had been betrayed in a garden, and buried in a garden. And as he turned round the screen of laurels, near the rock-face, he saw a woman hovering by the tomb, a woman in blue and yellow. She peeped again into the mouth of the hole, that was like a deep cupboard. But still there was nothing. And she wrung her hands and wept. And as she turned away, she saw the man in white, standing by the laurels, and she gave a cry, thinking it might be a spy, and she said:

'They have taken him away!'

So he said to her:

'Madeleine!'

Then she reeled as if she would fall, for she knew him. And he said to her:

'Madeleine! Do not be afraid. I am alive. They took me down too soon, so I came back to life. Then I was sheltered in a house.'

She did not know what to say, but fell at his feet to kiss them.

'Don't touch me, Madeleine,' he said. 'Not yet! I am not yet healed and in touch with men.'

So she wept because she did not know what to do. And he said:

'Let us go aside, among the bushes, where we can speak unseen.'

So in her blue mantle and her yellow robe, she followed him among the trees, and he sat down under a myrtle bush. And he said:

'I am not yet quite come to. Madeleine, what is to be done next?'

'Master!' she said. 'Oh, we have wept for you! And will you come back to us?'

'What is finished is finished, and for me the end is past,' he said. 'The stream will run till no more rains fill it, then it will dry up. For me, that life is over.'

'And will you give up your triumph?' she said sadly.

'My triumph,' he said, 'is that I am not dead. I have out-lived my mission and know no more of it. It is my triumph. I have survived the day and the death of my interference, and am still a man. I am young still, Madeleine, not even come to middle-age. I am glad all that is over. It had to be. But now I am glad it is over, and the day of my interference is done. The teacher and the saviour are dead in me; now I can go about my business, into my own single life.'

She heard him, and did not fully understand. But what he said made her feel disappointed.

'But you will come back to us?' she said, insisting.

'I don't know what I shall do,' he said. 'When I am healed, I shall know better. But my mission is over, and my teaching is finished, and death has saved me from my own salvation. Oh, Madeleine, I want to take my single way in life, which is my portion. My public life is over, the life of my self-importance. Now I can wait on life, and say nothing, and have no one betray me. I wanted to be greater than the limits of my hands and feet, so I brought betrayal on myself. And I know I wronged Judas, my poor Judas. For I have died, and now I know my own limits. Now I can live without striving to sway others any more. For my reach ends in my finger-tips, and my stride is no longer than the ends of my toes. Yet I would em-brace multitudes, I who have never truly embraced even one. But Judas and the high priests saved me from my own salva-tion, and soon I can turn to my destiny like a bather in the sea at dawn, who had just come down to the shore alone.'

'Do you want to be alone henceforward?' she asked. 'And was your mission nothing? Was it all untrue?'

'Nay!' he said. 'Neither were your lovers in the past nothing. They were much to you, but you took more than you gave. Then you came to me for salvation from your own excess. And I, in my mission, I too ran to excess. I gave more than I took, and that also is woe and vanity. So Pilate and the high priests saved me from my own excessive salvation. Don't run to excess now in living, Madeleine. It only means another death.'

She pondered bitterly, for the need for excessive giving was in her, and she could not bear to be denied.

'And will you not come back to us?' she said. 'Have you risen for yourself alone?'

He heard the sarcasm in her voice, and looked at her beautiful face which still was dense with excessive need for salvation from the woman she had been, the female who had caught men at her will. The cloud of necessity was on her, to be saved from the old, wilful Eve, who had embraced many men and taken more than she gave. Now the other doom was on her. She wanted to give without taking. And that, too, is hard, and cruel to the warm body.

'I have not risen from the dead in order to seek death again,' he said.

She glanced up at him, and saw the weariness settling again on his waxy face, and the vast disillusion in his dark eyes, and the underlying indifference. He felt her glance, and said to himself:

'Now my own followers will want to do me to death again, for having risen up different from their expectation.'

'But you will come to us, to see us, us who love you?' she said.

He laughed a little and said:

'Ah, yes.' Then he added: 'Have you a little money? Will you give me a little money? I owe it.'

She had not much, but it pleased her to give it to him.

'Do you think,' he said to her, 'that I might come and live with you in your house?'

She looked up at him with large blue eyes, that gleamed strangely.

'Now?' she said with peculiar triumph.

And he, who shrank now from triumph of any sort, his own or another's, said:

'Not now! Later, when I am healed, and ... and I am in touch with the flesh.'

The words faltered in him. And in his heart he knew he would never go to live in her house. For the flicker of triumph had gleamed in her eyes; the greed of giving. But she murmured in a humming rapture:

'Ah, you know I would give up everything to you.'

'Nay!' he said. 'I didn't ask that.'

A revulsion from all the life he had known came over him again, the great nausea of disillusion, and the spear-thrust through his bowels. He crouched under the myrtle bushes, without strength. Yet his eyes were open. And she looked at him again, and she saw that it was not the Messiah. The Messiah had not risen. The enthusiasm and the burning purity were gone, and the rapt youth. His youth was dead. This man was middle-aged and disillusioned, with a certain terrible indifference, and a resoluteness which love would never conquer. This was not the Master she had so adored, the young, flamy, unphysical exalter of her soul. This was nearer to the lovers she had known of old, but with a greater indifference to the personal issue, and a lesser susceptibility.

She was thrown out of the balance of her rapturous, anguished adoration. This risen man was the death of her dream.

'You should go now,' he said to her. 'Do not touch me, I am in death. I shall come again here, on the third day. Come if you will, at dawn. And we will speak again.'

She went away, perturbed and shattered. Yet as she went, her mind discarded the bitterness of the reality, and she conjured up rapture and wonder, that the Master was risen and was not dead. He was risen, the Saviour, the exalter, the wonder-worker! He was risen, but not as man; as pure God, who should not be touched by flesh, and who should be rapt away into Heaven. It was the most glorious and most ghostly of the miracles.

Meanwhile the man who had died gathered himself together at last, and slowly made his way to the peasants' house. He was glad to go back to them, and away from Madeleine and

138

his own associates. For the peasants had the inertia of earth and would let him rest, and as yet, would put no compulsion on him.

The woman was on the roof, looking for him. She was afraid that he had gone away. His presence in the house had become like gentle wine to her. She hastened to the door, to him.

'Where have you been?' she said. 'Why did you go away?'

'I have been to walk in a garden, and I have seen a friend, who gave me a little money. It is for you.'

He held out his thin hand, with the small amount of money, all that Madeleine could give him. The peasant's wife's eyes glistened, for money was scarce, and she said:

'Oh, master! And is it truly mine?'

'Take it!' he said. 'It buys bread, and bread brings life.'

So he lay down in the yard again, sick with relief at being alone again. For with the peasants he could be alone, but his own friends would never let him be alone. And in the safety of the yard, the young cock was dear to him, as it shouted in the helpless zest of life, and finished in the helpless humiliation of being tied by the leg. This day the ass stood swishing her tail under the shed. The man who had died lay down and turned utterly away from life, in the sickness of death in life.

But the woman brought wine and water, and sweetened cakes, and roused him, so that he ate a little, to please her. The day was hot, and as she crouched to serve him, he saw her breasts sway from her humble body, under her smock. He knew she wished he would desire her, and she was youngish, and not unpleasant. And he, who had never known a woman, would have desired her if he could. But he could not want her, though he felt gently towards her soft, crouching, humble body. But it was her thoughts, her consciousness, he could not mingle with. She was pleased with the money, and now she wanted to take more from him. She wanted the embrace of his body. But her little soul was hard, and short-sighted, and grasping, her body had its little greed, and no gentle reverence of the return gift. So he spoke a quiet, pleasant word to her and turned away. He could not touch the little, personal body,

the little, personal life of this woman, nor in any other. He
turned away from it without hesitation.

Risen from the dead, he had realized at last that the body,
too, has its little life, and beyond that, the greater life. He was
virgin, in recoil from the little, greedy life of the body. But
now he knew that virginity is a form of greed; and that the
body rises again to give and to take, to take and to give, un-
greedily. Now he knew that he had risen for the woman, or
women, who knew the greater life of the body, not greedy to
give, not greedy to take, and with whom he could mingle his
body. But having died, he was patient, knowing there was
time, an eternity of time. And he was driven by no greedy
desire, either to give himself to others, or to grasp anything
for himself. For he had died.

The peasant came home from work and said:

'Master, I thank you for the money. But we did not want it.
And all I have is yours.'

But the man who had died was sad, because the peasant
stood there in the little, personal body, and his eyes were
cunning and sparkling with the hope of greater rewards in
money later on. True, the peasant had taken him in free, and
had risked getting no reward. But the hope was cunning in
him. Yet even this was as men are made. So when the peasant
would have helped him to rise, for night had fallen, the man
who had died said:

'Don't touch me, brother. I am not yet risen to the Father.'

The sun burned with greater splendour, and burnished the
young cock brighter. But the peasant kept the string renewed,
and the bird was a prisoner. Yet the flame of life burned up to
a sharp point in the cock, so that it eyed askance and haughtily
the man who had died. And the man smiled and held the bird
dear, and he said to it:

'Surely thou art risen to the Father, among birds.'

And the young cock, answering, crowed.

When at dawn on the third morning the man went to the
garden, he was absorbed, thinking of the greater life of the
body, beyond the little, narrow, personal life. So he came
through the thick screen of laurel and myrtle bushes, near the

rock, suddenly, and he saw three women near the tomb. One was Madeleine, and one was the woman who had been his mother, and the third was a woman he knew, called Joan. He looked up, and saw them all, and they saw him, and they were all afraid.

He stood arrested in the distance, knowing they were there to claim him back, bodily. But he would in no wise return to them. Pallid, in the shadow of a grey morning that was blowing to rain, he saw them, and turned away. But Madeleine hastened towards him.

'I did not bring them,' she said. 'They have come of themselves. See, I have brought you money! ... Will you not speak to them?'

She offered him some gold pieces, and he took them, saying:

'May I have this money? I shall need it. I cannot speak to them, for I am not yet ascended to the Father. And I must leave you now.'

'Ah! Where will you go?' she cried.

He looked at her, and saw she was clutching for the man in him who had died and was dead, the man of his youth and his mission, of his chastity and his fear, of his little life, his giving without taking.

'I must go to my Father!' he said.

'And you will leave us? There is your mother!' she cried, turning round with the old anguish, which yet was sweet to her.

'But now I must ascend to my Father,' he said, and he drew back into the bushes, and so turned quickly, and went away, saying to himself:

'Now I belong to no one and have no connexion, and mission or gospel is gone from me. Lo! I cannot make even my own life, and what have I to save? ... I can learn to be alone.'

So he went back to the peasants' house, to the yard where the young cock was tied by the leg with a string. And he wanted no one, for it was best to be alone; for the presence of people made him lonely. The sun and the subtle salve of spring healed his wounds, even the gaping wound of disillusion through his bowels was closing up. And his need of men and women, his fever to have them and to be saved by them, this too was healing in him. Whatever came of touch between himself and the race of men, henceforth, should come without trespass or compulsion. For he said to himself:

'I tried to compel them to live, so they compelled me to die. It is always so, with compulsion. The recoil kills the advance. Now is my time to be alone.'

Therefore he went no more to the garden, but lay still and saw the sun, or walked at dusk across the olive slopes, among the green wheat, that rose a palm-breadth higher every sunny day. And always he thought to himself:

'How good it is to have fulfilled my mission, and to be beyond it. Now I can be alone, and leave all things to themselves, and the fig tree may be barren if it will, and the rich may be rich. My way is my own alone.'

So the green jets of leaves unspread on the fig tree, with the bright, translucent, green blood of the tree. And the young cock grew brighter, more lustrous with the sun's burnishing; yet always tied by the leg with a string. And the sun went down more and more in pomp, out of the gold and red-flushed air. The man who had died was aware of it all, and he thought:

'The Word is but the midge that bites at evening. Man is tormented with words like midges, and they follow him right into the tomb. But beyond the tomb they cannot go. Now I have passed the place where words can bite no more and the air is clear, and there is nothing to say, and I am alone within my own skin, which is the walls of all my domain.'

So he healed of his wounds, and enjoyed his immortality of being alive without fret. For in the tomb he had slipped that noose which we call care. For in the tomb he had left his striving self, which cares and asserts itself. Now his uncaring self healed and became whole within his skin, and he smiled to himself with pure aloneness, which is one sort of immortality.

Then he said to himself: 'I will wander the earth, and say nothing. For nothing is so marvellous as to be alone in the

phenomenal world, which is raging, and yet apart. And I have
not seen it, I was too much blinded by my confusion within
it. Now I will wander among the stirring of the phenomenal
world, for it is the stirring of all things among themselves
which leaves me purely alone.'

So he communed with himself, and decided to be a physician. Because the power was still in him to heal any man or
child who touched his compassion. Therefore he cut his hair
and his beard after the right fashion, and smiled to himself.
And he bought himself shoes, and the right mantle, and put
the right cloth over his head, hiding all the little scars. And the
peasant said:

'Master, will you go forth from us?'

'Yes, for the time is come for me to return to men.'

So he gave the peasant a piece of money, and said to him:

'Give me the cock that escaped and is now tied by the leg.
For he shall go forth with me.'

So for a piece of money the peasant gave the cock to the
man who had died, and at dawn the man who had died set out
into the phenomenal world, to be fulfilled in his own loneliness in the midst of it. For previously he had been too much
mixed up in it. Then he had died. Now he must come back, to
be alone in the midst. Yet even now he did not go quite alone,
for under his arm, as he went, he carried the cock, whose tail
fluttered gaily behind, and who craned his head excitedly, for
he too was adventuring out for the first time into the wider
phenomenal world, which is the stirring of the body of cocks
also. And the peasant woman shed a few tears, but then went
indoors, being a peasant, to look again at the pieces of money.
And it seemed to her, a gleam came out of the pieces of
money, wonderful.

The man who had died wandered on, and it was a sunny
day. He looked around as he went, and stood aside as the
pack-train passed by, towards the city. And he said to himself:

'Strange is the phenomenal world, dirty and clean together!
And I am the same. Yet I am apart! And life bubbles variously.
Why should I have wanted it to bubble all alike? What a pity I
preached to them! A sermon is so much more likely to cake

into mud, and to close the fountains, then is a psalm or a song.
I made a mistake. I understand that they executed me for
preaching to them. Yet they could not finally execute me, for
now I am risen in my own aloneness, and inherit the earth,
since I lay no claim on it. And I will be alone in the seethe of
all things; first and foremost, for ever, I shall be alone. But I
must toss this bird into the seethe of phenomena, for he must
ride his wave. How hot he is with life! Soon, in some place, I
shall leave him among the hens. And perhaps one evening I
shall meet a woman who can lure my risen body, yet leave me
my aloneness. For the body of my desire has died, and I am
not in touch anywhere. Yet how do I know! All at least is life.
And this cock gleams with bright aloneness, though he answers the lure of hens. And I shall hasten on to that village on
the hill ahead of me; already I am tired and weak, and want to
close my eyes to everything.'

Hastening a little with the desire to have finished going, he
overtook two men going slowly, and talking. And being soft-
footed, he heard they were speaking of himself. And he
remembered them, for he had known them in his life, the life
of his mission. So he greeted them, but did not disclose himself
in the dusk, and they did not know him. He said to them:

'What then of him who would be king, and was put to death
for it?'

They answered, suspiciously: 'Why ask you of him?'

'I have known him, and thought much about him,' he said.
So they replied: 'He has risen.'

'Yea! And where is he, and how does he live?'

'We know not, for it is not revealed. Yet he is risen, and in
a little while will ascend unto the Father.'

'Yea! And where then is his Father?'

'Know ye not? You are then of the Gentiles! The Father is
in Heaven, above the cloud and the firmament.'

'Truly? Then how will he ascend?'

'As Elijah the Prophet, he shall go up in a glory.'

'Even into the sky.'

'Into the sky.'

'Then is he not risen in the flesh?'

'He is risen in the flesh.'

'And will he take flesh up into the sky?'

'The Father in Heaven will take him up.'

The man who had died said no more, for his say was over, and words beget words, even as gnats. But the man asked him: 'Why do you carry a cock?'

'I am a healer,' he said, 'and the bird hath virtue.'

'You are not a believer?'

'Yea! I believe the bird is full of life and virtue.'

They walked on in silence after this, and he felt they disliked his answer. So he smiled to himself, for a dangerous phenomenon in the world is a man of narrow belief, who denies the right of his neighbour to be alone. And as they came to the outskirts of the village, the man who had died stood still in the gloaming and said in his old voice:

'Know ye me not?'

And they cried in fear: 'Master!'

'Yea!' he said, laughing softly. And he turned suddenly away, down a side lane, and was gone under the wall before they knew.

So he came to an inn where the asses stood in the yard. And he called for fritters, and they were made for him. So he slept under a shed. But in the morning he was wakened by a loud crowing, and his cock's voice ringing in his ears. So he saw the rooster of the inn walking forth to battle, with his hens, a goodly number, behind him. Then the cock of the man who had died sprang forth, and a battle began between the birds. The man of the inn ran to save his rooster, but the man who had died said:

'If my bird wins I will give him thee. And if he lose, thou shalt eat him.'

So the birds fought savagely, and the cock of the man who had died killed the common cock of the yard. Then the man who had died said to his young cock:

'Thou at least hast found thy kingdom, and the females to thy body. Thy aloneness can take on splendour, polished by the lure of thy hens.'

And he left his bird there, and went on deeper into the

phenomenal world, which is a vast complexity of entangle-ments and allurements. And he asked himself a last question:

'From what, and to what, could this infinite whirl be saved?'

So he went his way, and was alone. But the way of the world was past belief, as he saw the strange entanglement of passions and circumstance and compulsion everywhere, but always the dread insomnia of compulsion. It was fear, the ultimate fear of death, that made men mad. So always he must move on, for if he stayed, his neighbours wound the strangling of their fear and bullying round him. There was nothing he could touch, for all, in a mad assertion of the ego, wanted to put a compul-sion on him, and violate his intrinsic solitude. It was the mania of cities and societies and hosts, to lay a compulsion upon a man, upon all men. For men and women alike were mad with the egoistic fear of their own nothingness. And he thought of his own mission, how he had tried to lay the compulsion of love on all men. And the old nausea came back on him. For there was no contact without a subtle attempt to inflict a compulsion. And already he had been compelled even into death. The nausea of the old wound broke out afresh, and he looked again on the world with repulsion, dreading its mean contacts.

2

The wind came cold and strong from inland, from the invisible snows of Lebanon. But the temple, facing south and west, to-wards Egypt, faced the splendid sun of winter as he curved down towards the sea, the warmth and radiance flooded in between the pillars of painted wood. But the sea was invisible, because of the trees, though its dashing sounded among the hum of pines. The air was turning golden to afternoon. The woman who served Isis stood in her yellow robe, and looked up at the steep slopes coming down to the sea, where the olive trees silvered under the wind like water splashing. She was alone save for the goddess. And in the winter afternoon the light stood erect and magnificent off the invisible sea, filling the hills of the coast. She went towards the sun, through the grove of Mediterranean pine trees and evergreen oaks, in the midst of which the temple stood, on a little, tree-covered tongue of land between two bays.

It was only a very little way, and then she stood among the dry trunks of the outermost pines, on the rocks under which the sea smote and sucked, facing the open where the bright sun gloried in winter. The sea was dark, almost indigo, running away from the land, and crested with white. The hand of the wind brushed it strangely with shadow, as it brushed the olives of the slopes with silver. And there was no boat out.

The three boats were drawn high up on the steep shingle of the little bay, by the small grey tower. Along the edge of the shingle ran a high wall, inside which was a garden occupying the brief flat of the bay, then rising in terraces up the steep slope of the coast. And there, some little way up, within another wall, stood the low white villa, white and alone as the coast, overlooking the sea. But higher, much higher up, where the olives had given way to pine trees again, ran the coast road, keeping to the height to be above the gullies that came down to the bays.

Upon it all poured the royal sunshine of the January afternoon. Or rather, all was part of the great sun, glow and substance and immaculate loneliness of the sea, and pure brightness.

Crouching in the rocks above the dark water, which only swung up and down, two slaves, half naked, were dressing pigeons for the evening meal. They pierced the throat of a blue, live bird, and let the drops of blood fall into the heaving sea, with curious concentration. They were performing some sacrifice, or working some incantation. The woman of the temple, yellow and white and alone like a winter narcissus, stood between the pines of the small, humped peninsula where the temple secretly hid, and watched.

A black-and-white pigeon, vividly white, like a ghost escaped over the low dark sea, sped out, caught the wind, tilted, rode, soared, and swept over the pine trees, and wheeled away, a speck, inland. It had escaped. The priestess heard the cry of the boy slave, a garden slave of about seventeen. He raised his arms to heaven in anger as the pigeon wheeled away, naked and angry and young he held out his arms. Then he turned and seized the girl in an access of rage, and beat her with his fist that was stained with pigeon's blood. And she lay down with her face hidden, passive and quivering. The woman who owned them watched. And as she watched, she saw another onlooker, a stranger, in a low, broad hat, and a cloak of grey homespun, a dark bearded man standing on the little cause-way of a rock that was the neck of her temple peninsula. By the blowing of his dark-grey cloak she saw him. And he saw her, on the rocks like a white-and-yellow narcissus, because of the flutter of her white linen tunic, below the yellow mantle of wool. And both of them watched the two slaves.

The boy suddenly left off beating the girl. He crouched over her, touching her, trying to make her speak. But she lay quite inert, face down on the smoothed rock. And he put his arms round her and lifted her, but she slipped back to earth like one dead, yet far too quickly for anything dead. The boy, desper-ate, caught her by the hips and hugged her to him, turning her over there. There she seemed inert, all her fight was in her shoulders. He twisted her over, intent and unconscious, and pushed his hands between her thighs, to push them apart. And in an instant he was covering her in the blind, frightened frenzy of a boy's first passion. Quick and frenzied his young body quivered naked on hers, blind, for a minute. Then it lay quite still, as if dead.

And then, in terror, he peeped up. He peeped round, and drew slowly to his feet, adjusting his loin-rag. He saw the stranger, and then he saw, on the rocks beyond, the lady of Isis, his mistress. And as he saw her, his whole body shrank and cowed, and with a strange cringing motion he scuttled lamely towards the door in the wall.

The girl sat up and looked after him. When she had seen him disappear, she too looked round. And she saw the stran-ger and the priestess. Then with a sullen movement she turned away, as if she had seen nothing, to the four dead pigeons and the knife, which lay there on the rock. And she began to strip the small feathers, so that they rose on the wind like dust.

The priestess turned away. Slaves! Let the overseer watch them. She was not interested. She went slowly through the pines again, back to the temple, which stood in the sun in a small clearing at the centre of the tongue of land. It was a small temple of wood, painted all pink and white and blue, having at the front four wooden pillars rising like stems to the swollen lotus-bud of Egypt at the top, supporting the roof and open, spiky lotus-flowers of the outer frieze, which went round under the eaves. Two low steps of stone led up to the platform before the pillars, and the chamber behind the pillars was open. There a low stone altar stood, with a few embers in its hollow, and the dark stain of blood in its end groove.

She knew her temple so well, for she had built it at her own expense, and tended it for seven years. There it stood, pink and white, like a flower in the little clearing, backed by blackish evergreen oaks; and the shadow of afternoon was already washing over its pillar bases.

She entered slowly, passing through to the dark inner chamber, lighted by a perfumed oil-flame. And once more she pushed shut the door, and once more she threw a few grains of incense on a brazier before the goddess, and once more she sat down before her goddess, in the almost-darkness, to muse, to go away into the dreams of the goddess.

It was Isis; but not Isis, Mother of Horus. It was Isis Bereaved, Isis in Search. The goddess, in painted marble, lifted her face and strode, one thigh forward, through the frail fluting of her robe, in the anguish of bereavement and of search. She was looking for the fragments of the dead Osiris, dead and scattered asunder, dead, torn apart, and thrown in fragments over the wide world. And she must find his hands and his feet, his heart, his thighs, his head, his belly, she must gather him together and fold her arms round the re-assembled body till it became warm again, and roused to life, and could embrace her, and could fecundate her womb. And the strange rapture and anguish of search went on through the years, as she lifted her throat and her hollowed eyes looked inward, in the tormented ecstasy of seeking, and the delicate navel of her bud-like belly showed through the frail, girdled robe with the eternal asking, asking, of her search. And through the years she found him bit by bit, heart and head and limbs and body. And yet she had not found the last reality, the final clue to him, that alone could bring him really back to her. For she was Isis of the subtle lotus, the womb which waits submerged and in bud, waits for the touch of that other inward sun that streams its rays from the loins of the male Osiris.

This was the mystery the woman had served alone for seven years, since she was twenty, till now she was twenty-seven. Before, when she was young, she had lived in the world, in Rome, in Ephesus, in Egypt. For her father had been one of Anthony's captains and comrades, had fought with Anthony and had stood with him when Caesar was murdered, and through to the days of shame. Then he had come again across to Asia, out of favour with Rome, and had been killed in the mountains beyond Lebanon. The widow, having no favour to hope for from Octavius, had retired to her small property on the coast under Lebanon, taking her daughter from the world, a girl of nineteen, beautiful but unmarried.

When she was young the girl had known Caesar, and had shrunk from his eagle-like rapacity. The golden Anthony had sat with her many a half-hour, in the splendour of his great limbs and glowing manhood, and talked with her of the philosophies and the gods. For he was fascinated as a child by the gods, though he mocked at them, and forgot them in his own vanity. But he said to her:

'I have sacrificed two doves for you, to Venus, for I am afraid you make no offering to the sweet goddess. Beware you will offend her. Come, why is the flower of you so cool within? Does never a ray nor a glance find its way through? Ah, come, a maid should open to the sun, when the sun leans towards her to caress her.'

And the big, bright eyes of Anthony laughed down on her, bathing her in his glow. And she felt the lovely glow of his male beauty and his amorousness bathe all her limbs and her body. But it was as he said: the very flower of her womb was cool, was almost cold, like a bud in shadow of frost, for all the flooding of his sunshine. So Anthony, respecting her father, who loved her, had left her.

And it had always been the same. She saw many men, young and old. And on the whole, she liked the old ones best, for they talked to her still and sincere, and did not expect her to open like a flower to the sun of their maleness. Once she asked a philosopher: 'Are all women born to be given to men?' To which the old man answered slowly:

'Rare women wait for the re-born man. For the lotus, as you know, will not answer to all the bright heat of the sun. But she curves her dark, hidden head in the depths, and stirs not. Till, in the night, one of these rare, invisible suns that have been killed and shine no more, rises among the stars in unseen purple, and like the violet, sends its rare purple rays out into the night. To these the lotus stirs as to a caress, and rises upwards through the flood, and lifts up her bent head, and opens with an expansion such as no other flower knows, and spreads her sharp rays of bliss, and offers her soft, gold depths such as no other flower possesses, to the penetration of the flooding, violet-dark sun that has died and risen and makes no show. But for the golden brief day-suns of show, such as Anthony, and for the hard winter suns of power, such as Caesar, the lotus stirs not, nor will ever stir. Those will only tear open the bud. Ah, I tell you, wait for the re-born and wait for the bud to stir.'

So she had waited. For all the men were soldiers or politicians in the Roman spell, assertive, manly, splendid apparently but of an inward meanness, an inadequacy. And Rome and Egypt alike had left her alone, unroused. And she was a women to herself, she would not give herself for a surface glow, nor marry for reasons. She would wait for the lotus to stir.

And then, in Egypt, she had found Isis, in whom she spelled her mystery. She had brought Isis to the shores of Sidon, and lived with her in the mystery of search; whilst her mother, who loved affairs, controlled the small estate and the slaves with a free hand.

When the woman had roused from her muse and risen to perform the last brief ritual to Isis, she replenished the lamp and left the sanctuary, locking the door. In the outer world, the sun had already set, and twilight was chill among the humming trees, which hummed still, though the wind was abating.

A stranger in a dark, broad hat rose from the corner of the temple steps, holding his hat in the wind. He was dark-faced, with a black pointed beard. 'Oh, madam, whose shelter may I implore?' he said to the woman, who stood in her yellow mantle on a step above him, beside a pink-and-white painted pillar. Her face was rather long and pale, her dusky blonde hair was held under a thin gold net. She looked down on the vagabond with indifference. It was the same she had seen watching the slaves.

'Why come you down from the road?' she asked.

'I saw the temple like a pale flower on the coast, and would rest among the trees of the precincts, if the lady of the goddess permits.'

'It is Isis in Search,' she said, answering his first question.

'The goddess is great,' he replied.

She looked at him still with mistrust. There was a faint, remote smile in the dark eyes lifted to her, though the face was hollow with suffering. The vagabond divined her hesitation, and was mocking her.

'Stay here upon the steps,' she said. 'A slave will show you the shelter.'

'The lady of Egypt is gracious.'

She went down the rocky path of the humped peninsula in her gilded sandals. Beautiful were her ivory feet, beneath the white tunic, and above the saffron mantle her dusky-blonde head bent as with endless musings. A woman entangled in her own dream. The man smiled a little, half bitterly, and sat again on the step to wait, drawing his mantle round him, in the cold twilight.

At length a slave appeared, also in hodden grey.

'Seek ye the shelter of our lady?' he said insolently.

'Even so.'

'Then come.'

With the brusque insolence of a slave waiting on a vagabond, the young fellow led through the trees and down into a
little gully in the rock, where, almost in darkness, was a small
cave, with a litter of the tall heaths that grew on the waste
places of the coast, under the stone-pines. The place was
dark, but absolutely silent from the wind. There was still a
faint odour of goats.

'Here sleep!' said the slave. 'For the goats come no more
on this half-island. And there is water!' He pointed to a little
basin of rock where the maidenhair fern fringed a dripping
mouthful of water.

Having scornfully bestowed his patronage, the slave departed. The man who had died climbed out to the tip of the
peninsula, where the wave thrashed. It was rapidly getting
dark, and the stars were coming out. The wind was abating
for the night. Inland, the steep grooved up-slope was dark to
the long wavering outline of the crest against the translucent
sky. Only now and then a lantern flickered towards the
villa.

The man who had died went back to the shelter. There he
took bread from his leather pouch, dipped it in the water of the
tiny spring, and slowly ate. Having eaten and washed his
mouth, he looked once more at the bright stars in the pure
windy sky, then settled the heath for his bed. Having laid his
hat and his sandals aside, and put his pouch under his cheek
for a pillow, he slept, for he was very tired. Yet during the
night the cold woke him pinching wearily through his weariness. Outside was brilliantly starry, and still windy. He sat
and hugged himself in a sort of coma, and towards dawn went
to sleep again.

In the morning the coast was still chill in shadow, though
the sun was up behind the hills, when the woman came down
from the villa towards the goddess. The sea was fair and pale
blue, lovely in newness, and at last the wind was still. Yet the
waves broke white in the many rocks, and tore in the shingle

of the little bay. The woman came slowly towards her dream. Yet she was aware of an interruption.

As she followed the little neck of rock on to her peninsula, and climbed the slope between the trees to the temple, a slave came down and stood, making his obeisance. There was a faint insolence in his humility. 'Speak!' she said.

'Lady, the man is there, he still sleeps. Lady, may I speak?'

'Speak!' she said, repelled by the fellow.

'Lady, the man is an escaped malefactor.'

The slave seemed to triumph in imparting the unpleasant news.

'By what sign?'

'Behold his hands and feet! Will the lady look on him?'

'Lead on!'

The slave led quickly over the mound of the hill down to the tiny ravine. There he stood aside, and the woman went into the crack towards the cave. Her heart beat a little. Above all, she must preserve her temple inviolate.

The vagabond was asleep with his cheek on his scrip, his mantle wrapped round him, but his bare, soiled feet curling side by side, to keep each other warm, and his hand lying clenched in sleep. And in the pale skin of his feet usually covered by sandal-straps, she saw the scars, and in the palm of the loose hand.

She had no interest in men, particularly in the servile class. Yet she looked at the sleeping face. It was worn, hollow, and rather ugly. But, a true priestess, she saw the other kind of beauty in it, the sheer stillness of the deeper life. There was even a sort of majesty in the dark brows, over the still, hollow cheeks. She saw that his black hair, left long, in contrast to the Roman fashion, was touched with grey at the temples, and the black pointed beard had threads of grey. But that must be suffering or misfortune, for the man was young. His dusky skin had the silvery glisten of youth still.

There was a beauty of much suffering, and the strange calm candour of finer life in the whole delicate ugliness of the face. For the first time, she was touched on the quick at the sight of a man, as if the tip of a fine flame of living had touched her.

It was the first time. Men had roused all kinds of feeling in her, but never had touched her with the flame-tip of life.

She went back under the rock to where the slave waited.

'Know!' she said. 'This is no malefactor, but a free citizen of the east. Do not disturb him. But when he comes forth, bring him to me; tell him I would speak with him.'

She spoke coldly, for she found slaves invariably repellent, a little repulsive. They were so embedded in the lesser life, and their appetites and their small consciousness were a little disgusting. So she wrapped her dream round her and went to the temple, where a slave girl brought winter roses and jasmine for the altar. But today, even in her ministrations, she was disturbed.

The sun rose over the hill, sparkling, the light fell triumphantly on the little pine-covered peninsula of the coast, and on the pink temple, in the pristine newness. The man who had died woke up, and put on his sandals. He put on his hat too, slung his scrip under his mantle, and went out, to see the morning in all its blue and its new gold. He glanced at the little yellow-and-white narcissus sparkling gaily in the rocks. And he saw the slave waiting for him like a menace.

'Master!' said the slave. 'Our lady would speak with you at the house of Isis.'

'It is well,' said the wanderer.

He went slowly, staying to look at the pale blue sea like a flower in unruffled bloom, and the white fringes among the rocks, like white rock-flowers, the hollow slopes sheering up high from the shore, grey with olive trees and green with bright young wheat, and set with the white, small villa. All fair and pure in the January morning.

The sun fell on the corner of the temple, he sat down on the step in the sunshine, in the infinite patience of waiting. He had come back to life, but not the same life that he had left, the life of little people and the little day. Re-born, he was in the other life, the greater day of the human consciousness. And he was alone and apart from the little day, and out of contact with the daily people. Not yet had he accepted the irrevocable *noli me tangere* which separates the re-born from the vulgar. The separation was absolute, as yet here at the temple he felt peace, the hard, bright pagan peace with hostility of slaves beneath.

The woman came into the dark inner doorway of the temple from the shrine, and stood there, hesitating. She could see the dark figure of the man, sitting in that terrible stillness that was portentous to her, had something almost menacing in its patience.

She advanced across the outer chamber of the temple, and the man, becoming aware of her, stood up. She addressed him in Greek, but he said:

'Madam, my Greek is limited. Allow me to speak vulgar Syrian.'

'Whence come you? Whither go you?' she asked, with a hurried preoccupation of a priestess.

'From the east beyond Damascus – and I go west as the road goes,' he replied slowly.

She glanced at him with sudden anxiety and shyness.

'But why do you have the marks of a malefactor?' she asked abruptly.

'Did the Lady of Isis spy upon me in my sleep?' he asked, with a grey weariness.

'The slave warned me – your hands and feet –' she said.

He looked at her. Then he said:

'Will the Lady of Isis allow me to bid her farewell, and go up to the road?'

The wind came in a sudden puff, lifting his mantle and his hat. He put up his hand to hold the brim, and she saw again the thin brown hand with its scar.

'See! The scar!' she said, pointing.

'Even so!' he said. 'But farewell, and to Isis my homage and my thanks for sleep.'

He was going. But she looked up at him with her wondering blue eyes.

'Will you not look at Isis?' she said, with sudden impulse. And something stirred in him, like pain.

'Where then?' he said.

'Come!'

He followed her into the inner shrine, into the almost-darkness. When his eyes got used to the faint glow of the lamp, he saw the goddess striding like a ship, eager in the swirl of her gown, and he made his obeisance.

'Great is Isis!' he said. 'In her search she is greater than death. Wonderful is such walking in a woman, wonderful the goal. All men praise thee, Isis, thou greater than the mother unto man.'

The woman of Isis heard, and threw incense on the brazier. Then she looked at the man.

'Is it well with thee here?' she asked him. 'Has Isis brought thee home to herself?'

He looked at the priestess in wonder and trouble.

'I know not,' he said.

But the woman was pondering that this was the lost Osiris. She felt in the quick of her soul. And her agitation was intense.

He would not stay in the close, dark, perfumed shrine. He went out again to the morning, to the cold air. He felt something approaching to touch him, and all his flesh was still woven with pain and the wild commandment: *Noli me tangere!* Touch me not! Oh, don't touch me!

The woman followed into the open with timid eagerness. He was moving away.

'Oh, stranger, do not go! Oh, stay a while with Isis!'

He looked at her, at her face open like a flower, as if a sun had risen in her soul. And again his loins stirred.

'Would you detain me, girl of Isis?' he said.

'Stay! I am sure you are Osiris!' she said.

He laughed suddenly. 'Not yet!' he said. Then he looked at her wistful face. 'But I will sleep another night in the cave of the goats, if Isis wills it,' he added.

She put her hands together with a priestess's childish happiness.

'Ah! Isis will be glad!' she said.

So he went down to the shore in great trouble, saying to himself: 'Shall I give myself into this touch? Shall I give myself into this touch? Men have tortured me to death with their touch. Yet this girl of Isis is a tender flame of healing. I am a physician, yet I have no healing like the flame of this tender girl. The flame of this tender girl! Like the first pale crocus of the spring. How could I have been blind to the healing and the bliss in the crocus-like body of a tender woman! Ah, tenderness! More terrible and lovely than the death I died –'

He pried small shell-fish from the rocks, and ate them with relish and wonder for the simple taste of the sea. And inwardly he was tremulous, thinking: 'Dare I come into touch? For this is farther than death. I have dared to let them lay hands on me and put me to death. But dare I come into this tender touch of life? Oh, this is harder –'

But the woman went into the shrine again, and sat rapt in pure muse, through the long hours, watching the swirling stride of the yearning goddess, and the navel of the bud-like belly, like a seal on the virgin urge of the search. And she gave herself to the woman-flow and to the urge of Isis in Search.

Towards sundown she went on the peninsula to look for him. And she found him gone towards the sun, as she had gone the day before, and sitting on the pine-needles at the foot of the tree, where she had stood when first she saw him. Now she approached tremulously and slowly, afraid lest he did not want her. She stood near him unseen, till suddenly he glanced up at her from under his broad hat, and saw the westering sun on her netted hair. He was startled, yet he expected her.

'Is that your home?' he said, pointing to the white, low villa on the slope of olives.

'It is my mother's house. She is a widow, and I am her only child.'

'And are these all her slaves?'

'Except those that are mine.'

Their eyes met for a moment.

'Will you too sit to see the sun go down?' he said.

He had not risen to speak to her. He had known too much pain. So she sat on the dry brown pine-needles, gathering her saffron mantle round her knees. A boat was coming in, out of the open glow into the shadow of the bay, and slaves were lifting small nets, their babble coming off the surface of the water.

'And this is home to you,' he said.

'But I serve Isis in Search,' she replied.

He looked at her. She was like a soft, musing cloud, somehow remote. His soul smote him with passion and compassion.

'Mayst thou find thy desire, maiden,' he said, with sudden earnestness.

'And art thou not Osiris?' she asked.

He flushed suddenly.

'Yes, if thou wilt heal me!' he said. 'For the death aloofness is still upon me, and I cannot escape it.'

She looked at him for a moment in fear from the soft blue sun of her eyes. Then she lowered her head, and they sat in silence in the warmth and glow of the western sun: the man who had died, and the woman of the pure search.

The sun was curving down to the sea, in grand winter splendour. It fell on the twinkling, naked bodies of the slaves, with their ruddy broad hams and their small black heads, as they ran spreading the nets on the pebble beach. The all-tolerant Pan watched over them. All-tolerant Pan should be their god for ever.

The woman rose as the sun's rim dipped, saying:

'If you will stay, I shall send down victual and covering.'

'The lady your mother, what will she say?'

The woman of Isis looked at him strangely, but with a tinge of misgiving.

'It is my own,' she said.

'It is good,' he said, smiling faintly and foreseeing difficulties.

He watched her go, with her absorbed, strange motion of the self-dedicate. Her dun head was a little bent, the white linen swung about her ivory ankles. And he saw the naked slaves stand to look at her, with a certain wonder, and even a certain mischief. But she passed intent through the door in the wall, on the bay.

The man who had died sat on at the foot of the tree overlooking the strand, for on the little shore everything happened. At the small stream which ran in round the corner of the property wall, women slaves were still washing linen, and now and again came the hollow chock! chock! chock! as they beat it against the smooth stones in the dark little hollow of the pool. There was a smell of olive refuse on the air; and sometimes still the faint rumble of the grindstone that was milling the olives, inside the garden, and the sound of the slave calling to the ass at the mill. Then through the doorway a woman stepped, a grey-haired woman in a mantle of whitish wool, and there followed her a bare-headed man in a toga, a Roman: probably her steward or overseer. They stood on the high shingle above the sea, and cast round a rapid glance. The broad-hammed, ruddy-bodied slaves bent absorbed and abject over the nets, picking them clean, the women washing linen thrust their palms with energy down on the wash, the old slave bent absorbed at the water's edge, washing the fish and the polyps of the catch. And the woman and the overseer saw it all in one glance. They also saw, seated at the foot of the tree on the rocks of the peninsula, the strange man silent and alone. And the man who had died saw that they spoke of him. Out of the little sacred world of the peninsula he looked on the common world, and saw it still hostile.

The sun was touching the sea, across the tiny bay stretched the shadow of the opposite humped headland. Over the shingle, now blue and cold in shadow, the elderly woman trod heavily, in shadow too, to look at the fish spread in the flat basket of the old man crouching at the water's edge: a naked old slave with fat hips and shoulders, on whose soft, fairish-orange body the last sun twinkled, then died. The old slave continued cleaning the fish absorbedly, not looking up: as if the lady were the shadow of twilight falling on him.

Then from the gateway stepped two slave-girls with flat baskets on their heads, and from one basket the terra-cotta wine-jar and the oil-jar poked up, leaning slightly. Over the massive shingle, under the wall, came the girls, and the woman of Isis in her saffron mantle stepped in twilight after them. Out at sea, the sun still shone. Here was shadow. The mother with grey head stood at the sea's edge and watched the daughter, all yellow and white, with dun blonde head, swinging unseeing and unheeding after the slave-girls, towards the neck of rock of the peninsula; the daughter, travelling in her absorbed other-world. And not moving from her place, the elderly mother watched that procession of three file up the rise of the headland, between the trees, and disappear, shut in by trees. No slave had lifted a head to look. The grey-haired woman still watched the trees where her daughter had disappeared. Then she glanced again at the foot of the tree, where the man who had died was still sitting, inconspicuous now, for the sun had left him; and only the far blade of the sea shone bright. It was evening. Patience! Let destiny move!

The mother plodded with a stamping stride up the shingle: not long and swinging and rapt, like the daughter, but short and determined. Then down the rocks opposite came two naked slaves trotting with huge bundles of dark green on their shoulders, so their broad, naked legs twinkled underneath like insects' legs, and their heads were hidden. They came trotting across the shingle, heedless and intent on their way, when suddenly the man, the Roman-looking overseer, addressed them, and they stopped dead. They stood invisible under their loads, as if they might disappear altogether, now they were arrested. Then a hand came out and pointed to the peninsula. Then the two green-heaped slaves trotted on, towards the temple precincts. The grey-haired woman joined the man, and slowly the two passed through the door again, from the shingle of the sea to the property of the villa. Then the old, fat-shouldered slave rose, pallid in the shadow, with his tray of fish from the sea, and the woman rose from the pool, dusky and alive, piling the wet linen in a heap on to the flat baskets, and the slaves who had cleaned the net gathered its whitish folds together. And the old slave with the fish-basket on his shoulder, and the women-slaves with the heaped baskets of wet linen on their heads, and the two slaves with the folded net, and the slave with oars on his shoulders, and the boy with the folded sail on his arm, gathered in a naked group near the door, and the man who had died heard the low buzz of their chatter. Then as the wind wafted cold, they began to pass through the door.

LOVE AMONG THE HAYSTACKS

It was the life of the little day, the life of little people. And the man who had died said to himself: 'Unless we encompass it in the greater day, and set the little life in the circle of the greater life, all is disaster.'

Even the tops of the hills were in shadow. Only the sky was still upwardly radiant. The sea was a vast milky shadow. The man who had died rose a little stiffly and turned into the grove.

There was no one at the temple. He went on to his lair in the rock. There, the slave-men had carried out the old heath of the bedding, swept the rock floor, and were spreading with nice art the myrtle, then the rougher heath, then the soft, bushy heath-tips on top, for a bed. Over it all they put a well-tanned white ox-skin. The maids had laid folded woollen covers at the head of the cave, and the wine-jar, the oil-jar, a terra-cotta drinking-cup and a basket containing bread, salt, cheese, dried figs, and eggs stood neatly arranged. There was also a little brazier of charcoal. The cave was suddenly full, and a dwelling-place.

The woman of Isis stood in the hollow by the tiny spring. Only one slave at a time could pass. The girl-slaves waited at the entrance to the narrow place. When the man who had died appeared, the woman sent the girls away. The men-slaves still arranged the bed, making the job as long as possible. But the woman of Isis dismissed them too. And the man who had died came to look at his house.

'Is it well?' the woman asked him.

'It is very well,' the man replied. 'But the lady, your mother, and he who is no doubt the steward, watched while the slaves brought the goods. Will they not oppose you?'

'I have my own portion! Can I not give of my own? Who is going to oppose me and the gods?' she said, with a certain soft fury, touched with exasperation. So that he knew that her mother would oppose her, and that the spirit of the little life would fight against the spirit of the greater. And he thought: 'Why did the woman of Isis relinquish her portion in the daily world? She should have kept her goods fiercely!'

'Will you eat and drink?' she said. 'On the ashes are warm

eggs. And I will go up to the meal at the villa. But in the second hour of the night I shall come down to the temple. O, then, will you come too to Isis?' She looked at him, and a queer glow dilated her eyes. This was her dream, and it was greater than herself. He could not bear to thwart her or hurt her in the least thing now. She was in the full glow of her woman's mystery.

'Shall I wait at the temple?' he said.

'O, wait at the second hour and I shall come.' He heard the humming supplication in her voice and his fibres quivered.

'But the lady, your mother?' he said gently.

The woman looked at him, startled.

'She will not thwart me!' she said.

So he knew that the mother would thwart the daughter, for the daughter had left her goods in the hands of her mother, who would hold fast to this power.

But she went, and the man who had died lay reclining on his couch, and ate the eggs from the ashes, and dipped his bread in oil, and ate it, for his flesh was dry: and he mixed wine and water, and drank. And so he lay still, and the lamp made a small bud of light.

He was absorbed and enmeshed in new sensations. The woman of Isis was lovely to him, not so much in form as in the wonderful womanly glow of her. Suns beyond suns had dipped her in mysterious fire, the mysterious fire of a potent woman, and to touch her was like touching the sun. Best of all was her tender desire for him, like sunshine, so soft and still.

'She is like sunshine upon me,' he said to himself, stretching his limbs. 'I have never before stretched my limbs in such sunshine, as her desire for me. The greatest of all gods granted me this.'

At the same time he was haunted by the fear of the outer world. 'If they can, they will kill us,' he said to himself. 'But there is a law of the sun which protects us.'

And again he said to himself: 'I have risen naked and branded. But if I am naked enough for this contact, I have not died in vain. Before I was clogged.'

He rose and went out. The night was chill and starry, and of a great wintry splendour. 'There are destinies of splendour,' he said to the night, 'after all our doom of littleness and meanness and pain.'

So he went up silently to the temple, and waited in darkness against the inner wall, looking out on a grey darkness, stars, and rims of trees. And he said again to himself: 'There are destinies of splendour, and there is a greater power.'

So at last he saw the light of her silk lanthorn swinging, coming intermittent between the trees, yet coming swiftly. She was alone, and near, the light softly swishing on her mantle-hem. And he trembled with fear and with joy, saying to himself: 'I am almost more afraid of this touch than I was of death. For I am more nakedly exposed to it.'

'I am here, Lady of Isis,' he said softly out of the dark.

'Ah!' she cried, in fear also, yet in rapture. For she was given to her dream.

She unlocked the door of the shrine, and he followed after her. Then she latched the door shut again. The air inside was warm and close and perfumed. The man who had died stood by the closed door and watched the woman. She had come first to the goddess. And dim-lit, the goddess-statue stood surging forward, a little fearsome like a great woman-presence urging.

The priestess did not look at him. She took off her saffron mantle and laid it on a low couch. In the dim light she was bare armed, in her girdled white tunic. But she was still hiding herself away from him. He stood back in shadow and watched her softly fan the brazier and fling on incense. Faint clouds of sweet aroma arose on the air. She turned to the statue in the ritual of approach, softly swaying forward with a slight lurch, like a moored boat, tipping towards the goddess.

He watched the strange rapt woman, and he said to himself: 'I must leave her alone in her rapture, her female mysteries.' So she tipped in her strange forward-swaying rhythm before the goddess. Then she broke into a murmur of Greek, which he could not understand. And, as she murmured, her swaying softly subsided, like a boat on a sea that grows still. And as he watched her, he saw her soul in its aloneness, and its female difference. He said to himself: 'How different she is from me, how strangely different! She is afraid of me, and my male difference. She is getting herself naked and clear of her fear. How sensitive and softly alive she is, with a life so different from mine! How beautiful with a soft, strange courage, of life, so different from my courage of death! What a beautiful thing, like the heart of a rose, like the core of a flame. She is making herself completely penetrable. Ah! how terrible to fail her, or to trespass on her!'

She turned to him, her face glowing from the goddess.

'You are Osiris, aren't you?' she said naïvely.

'If you will,' he said.

'Will you let Isis discover you? Will you not take off your things?'

He looked at the woman, and lost his breath. And his wounds, and especially the death-wound through his belly, began to cry again.

'It has hurt so much!' he said. 'You must forgive me if I am still held back.'

But he took off his cloak and his tunic and went naked towards the idol, his breast panting with the sudden terror of overwhelming pain, memory of overwhelming pain, and grief too bitter.

'They did me to death!' he said in excuse of himself, turning his face to her for a moment.

And she saw the ghost of the death in him as he stood there thin and stark before her, and suddenly she was terrified, and she felt robbed. She felt the shadow of the grey, grisly wing of death triumphant.

'Ah, Goddess,' he said to the idol in the vernacular. 'I would be so glad to live, if you would give me my clue again.'

For her again he felt desperate, faced by the demand of life, and burdened still by his death.

'Let me anoint you!' the woman said to him softly. 'Let me anoint the scars! Show me, and let me anoint them!'

He forgot his nakedness in this re-evoked old pain. He sat on the edge of the couch, and she poured a little ointment into the palm of his hand. And as she chafed his hand, it all came back, the nails, the holes, the cruelty, the unjust cruelty against him who had offered only kindness. The agony of injustice and cruelty came over him again, as in his death-hour. But she chafed the palm, murmuring: 'What was torn becomes a new flesh, what was a wound is full of fresh life; this scar is the eye of the violet.'

And he could not help smiling at her, in her naïve priestess's absorption. This was her dream, and he was only a dream-object to her. She would never know or understand what he was. Especially she would never know the death that was gone before in him. But what did it matter? She was different. She was woman: her life and her death were different from him. Only she was good to him.

When she chafed his feet with oil and tender, tender healing, he could not refrain from saying to her:

'Once a woman washed my feet with tears, and wiped them with her hair, and poured on precious ointment.'

The woman of Isis looked up at him from her earnest work, interrupted again.

'Were they hurt then?' she said. 'Your feet?'

'No, no! It was while they were whole.'

'And did you love her?'

'Love had passed in her. She only wanted to serve,' he replied. 'She had been a prostitute.'

'And did you let her serve you?' she asked.

'Yea.'

'Did you let her serve you with the corpse of her love?'

'Ay!'

Suddenly it dawned on him: I asked them all to serve me with the corpse of their love. And in the end I offered them only the corpse of my love. This is my body – take and eat – my corpse –

A vivid shame went through him. 'After all,' he thought, 'I wanted them to love with dead bodies. If I had kissed Judas with live love, perhaps he would never have kissed me with death. Perhaps he loved me in the flesh, and I will that he should love me bodylessly, with the corpse of love –'

There dawned on him the reality of the soft, warm love

which is in touch, and which is full of delight. 'And I told them, blessed are they that mourn,' he said to himself. 'Alas, if I mourned even this woman here, now I am in death, I should have to remain dead, and I want so much to live. Life has brought me to this woman with warm hands. And her touch is more to me now than all my words. For I want to live –'

'Go then to the goddess!' she said softly, gently pushing him towards Isis. And as he stood there dazed and naked as an unborn thing, he heard the woman murmuring to the goddess, murmuring, murmuring with a plaintive appeal. She was stooping now, looking at the scar in the soft flesh of the socket of his side, a scar deep and like an eye sore with endless weeping, just in the soft socket above the hip. It was here that his blood had left him, and his essential seed. The woman was trembling softly and murmuring in Greek. And he in the recurring dismay of having died, and in the anguished perplexity of having tried to force life, felt his wounds crying aloud, and the deep places of the body howling again: 'I have been murdered, and I lent myself to murder. They murdered me, but I lent myself to murder –'

The woman, silent now, but quivering, laid oil in her hand and put her palm over the wound in his right side. He winced, and the wound absorbed his life again, as thousands of times before. And in the dark, wild pain and panic of his consciousness rang only one cry: 'Oh, how can she take this death out of me? She can never know! She can never understand! She can never equal it! ...'

In silence, she softly rhythmically chafed the scar with oil. Absorbed now in her priestess's task, softly, softly gathering power, while the vitals of the man howled in panic. But as she gradually gathered power, and passed in a girdle round him to the opposite scar, gradually warmth began to take the place of the cold terror, and he felt: 'I am going to be warm again, and I am going to be whole! I shall be warm like the morning. I shall be a man. It doesn't need understanding. It needs newness. She brings me newness –'

And he listened to the faint, ceaseless wail of distress of his wounds, sounding as if for ever under the horizons of his consciousness. But the wail was growing dim, more dim.

He thought of the woman toiling over him: 'She does not know! She does not realize the death in me. But she has another consciousness. She comes to me from the opposite end of the night.'

Having chafed all his lower body with oil, having worked with her slow intensity of a priestess, so that the sound of his wounds grew dimmer and dimmer, suddenly she put her breast against the wound in his left side, and her arms round him, folding over the wound in his right side, and she pressed him to her, in a power of living warmth, like the folds of a river. And the wailing died out altogether, and there was a stillness, and darkness in his soul, unbroken, dark stillness, wholeness.

Then slowly, slowly, in the perfect darkness of his inner man, he felt the stir of something coming. A dawn, a new sun. A new sun was coming up in him, in the perfect inner darkness of himself. He waited for it breathless, quivering with a fearful hope ... 'Now I am not myself. I am something new ...'

And as it rose, he felt, with a cold breath of disappointment, the girdle of the living woman slip down from him, the warmth and the glow slipped from him, leaving him stark. She crouched, spent, at the feet of the goddess, hiding her face.

Stooping, he laid his hand softly on her warm, bright shoulder, and the shock of desire went through him, shock after shock, so that he wondered if it were another sort of death: but full of magnificence.

Now all his consciousness was there in the crouching, hidden woman. He stooped beside her and caressed her softly, blindly, murmuring inarticulate things. And his death and his passion of sacrifice were all as nothing to him now, he knew only the crouching fullness of the woman there, the soft white rock of life ... 'On this rock I built my life.' The deep-folded, penetrable rock of the living woman! The woman, hiding her face. Himself bending over, powerful and new like dawn.

He crouched to her, and he felt the blaze of his manhood and his power rise up in his loins, magnificent.

'I am risen!'

Magnificent, blazing indomitable in the depths of his loins, his own sun dawned, and sent its fire running along his limbs, so that his face shone unconsciously.

He untied the string on the linen tunic and slipped the garment down, till he saw the white glow of her white-gold breasts. And he touched them, and he felt his life go molten. 'Father!' he said, 'why did you hide this from me?' And he touched her with the poignancy of wonder, and the marvellous piercing transcendence of desire. 'Lo!' he said, 'this is beyond prayer.' It was the deep, interfolded warmth, warmth living and penetrable, the woman, the heart of the rose! My mansion is the intricate warm rose, my joy is this blossom!

She looked up at him suddenly, her face like a lifted light, wistful, tender, her eyes like many wet flowers. And he drew her to his breast with a passion of tenderness and consuming desire, and the last thought: 'My hour is upon me, I am taken unawares –'

So he knew her, and was one with her.

Afterwards, with a dim wonder, she touched the great scars in his sides with her finger-tips, and said:

'But they no longer hurt?'

'They are suns!' he said. 'They shine from your torch. They are my atonement with you.'

And when they left the temple, it was the coldness before dawn. As he closed the door, he looked again at the goddess, and he said: 'Lo, Isis is a kindly goddess; and full of tenderness. Great gods are warm-hearted, and have tender goddesses.'

The woman wrapped herself in her mantle and went home in silence, sightless, brooding like the lotus softly shutting again, with its gold core full of fresh life. She saw nothing, for her own petals were a sheath to her. Only she thought: 'I am full of Osiris. I am full of the risen Osiris! ...'

But the man looked at the vivid stars before dawn, as they rained down to the sea, and the dog-star green towards the sea's rim. And he thought: 'How plastic it is, how full of curves and folds like an invisible rose of dark-petalled openness that shows where the dew touches its darkness! How full it is, and great beyond all gods. How it leans around me, and I am part of it, the great rose of Space. I am like a grain of its perfume, and the woman is a grain of its beauty. Now the world is one flower of many petalled darknesses, and I am in its perfume as in a touch.'

So, in the absolute stillness and fullness of touch, he slept in his cave while the dawn came. And after the dawn, the wind rose and brought a storm, with cold rain. So he stayed in his cave in the peace and the delight of being in touch, delighting to hear the sea, and the rain on the earth, and to see one white-and-gold narcissus bowing wet, and still wet. And he said: 'This is the great atonement, the being in touch. The grey sea and the rain, the wet narcissus and the woman I wait for, the invisible Isis and the unseen sun are all in touch, and at one.'

He waited at the temple for the woman, and she came in the rain. But she said to him:

'Let me sit awhile with Isis. And come to me, will you come to me, in the second hour of night?'

So he went back to the cave and lay in stillness and in the joy of being in touch, waiting for the woman who would come with the night, and consummate again the contact. Then when night came the woman came, and came gladly, for her great yearning, too, was upon her, to be in touch, to be in touch with him, nearer.

So the days came, and the nights came, and days came again, and the contact was perfected and fulfilled. And he said: 'I will ask her nothing, not even her name, for a name would set her apart.'

And she said to herself: 'He is Osiris. I wish to know no more.'

Plum blossom blew from the trees, the time of the narcissus was past, anemones lit up the ground and were gone, the perfume of bean-field was in the air. All changed, the blossom of the universe changed its petals and swung round to look another way. The spring was fulfilled, a contact was established, the man and the woman were fulfilled of one another, and departure was in the air.

One day he met her under the trees, when the morning sun was hot, and the pines smelled sweet, and on the hills the last pear blossom was scattering. She came slowly towards him, and in her gentle lingering, her tender hanging back from him, he knew a change in her.

'Hast thou conceived?' he asked her.

'Why?' she said.

'Thou art like a tree whose green leaves follow the blossom, full of sap. And there is a withdrawing about thee.'

'It is so,' she said. 'I am with young by thee. Is it good?'

'Yes!' he said. 'How should it not be good? So the nightingale calls no more from the valley-bed. But where wilt thou bear the child, for I am naked of all but life?'

'We will stay here,' she said.

'But the lady, your mother?'

A shadow crossed her brow. She did not answer.

'What when she knows?' he said.

'She begins to know.'

'And would she hurt you?'

'Ah, not me! What I have is all my own. And I shall be big with Osiris ... But thou, do you watch her slaves.'

She looked at him, and the peace of her maternity was troubled by anxiety.

'Let not your heart be troubled!' he said. 'I have died the death once.'

So he knew the time was come again for him to depart. He would go alone, with his destiny. Yet not alone, for the touch would be upon him, even as he left his touch on her. And invisible suns would go with him.

Yet he must go. For here on the bay the little life of jealously and property was resuming sway again, as the suns of passionate fecundity relaxed their sway. In the name of property, the widow and her slaves would seek to be revenged on him for the bread he had eaten, and the living touch he had established, the woman he had delighted in. But he said: 'Not twice! They shall not now profane the touch in me. My wits against theirs.'

So he watched. And he knew they plotted. So he moved from the little cave and found another shelter, a tiny cove of sand by the sea, dry and secret under the rocks.

He said to the woman:

'I must go now soon. Trouble is coming to me from the slaves. But I am a man, and the world is open. But what is between us is good, and is established. Be at peace. And when the nightingale calls again from your valley-bed, I shall come again, sure as spring.'

She said: 'O, don't go! Stay with me on half the island, and I will build a house for you and me under the pine trees by the temple, where we can live apart.'

Yet she knew that he would go. And even she wanted the coolness of her own air around her, and the release from anxiety.

'If I stay,' he said, 'they will betray me to the Romans and to their justice. But I will never be betrayed again. So when I am gone, live in peace with the growing child. And I shall come again: all is good between us, near or apart. The suns come back in their seasons: and I shall come again.'

'Do not go yet,' she said. 'I have set a slave to watch at the neck of the peninsula. Do not go yet, till the harm shows.'

But as he lay in his little cove, on a calm, still night, he heard the soft knock of oars, and the bump of a boat against the rock. So he crept out to listen. And he heard the Roman overseer say:

'Lead softly to the goat's den. And Lysippus shall throw the net over the malefactor while he sleeps, and we will bring him before justice, and the Lady of Isis shall know nothing of it ...'

The man who had died caught a whiff of flesh from the oiled and naked slaves as they crept up, then the faint perfume of the Roman. He crept nearer to the sea. The slave who sat in the boat sat motionless, holding the oars, for the sea was quite still. And the man who had died knew him.

So out of the deep cleft of a rock he said, in a clear voice:

'Art thou not that slave who possessed the maiden under the eyes of Isis? Art thou not the youth? Speak!'

The youth stood up in the boat in terror. His movement sent the boat bumping against the rock. The slave sprang out in wild fear, and fled up the rocks. The man who had died quickly seized the boat and stepped in, and pushed off. The oars were yet warm with the unpleasant warmth of the hands of the slaves. But the man pulled slowly out, to get into the current which set down the coast, and would carry him in silence. The high coast was utterly dark against the starry night. There was no glimmer from the peninsula: the priestess came no more at night. The man who had died rowed slowly on, with the current, and laughed to himself: 'I have sowed the seed of my life and my resurrection, and put my touch for ever upon the choice woman of this day, and I carry her perfume in my flesh like essence of roses. She is dear to me in the middle of my being. But the gold and flowing serpent is coiling up again, to sleep at the root of my tree.'

'So let the boat carry me. Tomorrow is another day.'

READ MORE IN PENGUIN

In every corner of the world, on every subject under the sun, Penguin represents quality and variety – the very best in publishing today.

For complete information about books available from Penguin – including Puffins, Penguin Classics and Arkana – and how to order them, write to us at the appropriate address below. Please note that for copyright reasons the selection of books varies from country to country.

In the United Kingdom: Please write to *Dept. JC, Penguin Books Ltd, FREEPOST, West Drayton, Middlesex UB7 0BR*

If you have any difficulty in obtaining a title, please send your order with the correct money, plus ten per cent for postage and packaging, to *PO Box No. 11, West Drayton, Middlesex UB7 0BR*

In the United States: Please write to *Penguin USA Inc., 375 Hudson Street, New York, NY 10014*

In Canada: Please write to *Penguin Books Canada Ltd, 10 Alcorn Avenue, Suite 300, Toronto, Ontario M4V 3B2*

In Australia: Please write to *Penguin Books Australia Ltd, 487 Maroondah Highway, Ringwood, Victoria 3134*

In New Zealand: Please write to *Penguin Books (NZ) Ltd, 182–190 Wairau Road, Private Bag, Takapuna, Auckland 9*

In India: Please write to *Penguin Books India Pvt Ltd, 706 Eros Apartments, 56 Nehru Place, New Delhi 110 019*

In the Netherlands: Please write to *Penguin Books Netherlands B.V., Keizersgracht 231 NL–1016 DV Amsterdam*

In Germany: Please write to *Penguin Books Deutschland GmbH, Friedrichstrasse 10–12, W–6000 Frankfurt/Main 1*

In Spain: Please write to *Penguin Books S. A., C. San Bernardo 117–6° E–28015 Madrid*

In Italy: Please write to *Penguin Italia s.r.l., Via Felice Casati 20, I–20124 Milano*

In France: Please write to *Penguin France S. A., 17 rue Lejeune, F–31000 Toulouse*

In Japan: Please write to *Penguin Books Japan, Ishikiribashi Building, 2–5–4, Suido, Tokyo 112*

In Greece: Please write to *Penguin Hellas Ltd, Dimocritou 3, GR–106 71 Athens*

In South Africa: Please write to *Longman Penguin Southern Africa (Pty) Ltd, Private Bag X08, Bertsham 2013*

READ MORE IN PENGUIN

D. H. LAWRENCE IN PENGUIN

D. H. Lawrence is acknowledged as one of the greatest writers of the twentieth century. Nearly all his works have been published by Penguin.

NOVELS

Aaron's Rod
The Lost Girl
The Rainbow
The Trespasser
Women in Love
The First Lady Chatterley
The Boy in the Bush

Lady Chatterley's Lover
The Plumed Serpent
Sons and Lovers
The White Peacock
Kangaroo
John Thomas and Lady Jane

SHORT STORIES

The Prussian Officer
Love Among the Haystacks
The Princess

England, My England
The Woman Who Rode Away
The Mortal Coil

Three Novellas: The Fox/The Ladybird/The Captain's Doll
St Mawr *and* The Virgin and the Gipsy
Selected Short Stories

TRAVEL BOOKS AND OTHER WORKS

Mornings in Mexico
Studies in Classic
   American Literature
Apocalypse

Fantasia of the Unconscious *and*
   Psychoanalysis and the
   Unconscious
D. H. Lawrence and Italy

POETRY

D. H. Lawrence: The Complete Poems
Edited and Introduced by Vivian de Sola Pinto and F. Warren Roberts